PLAIN ESCAPE

HUNTERS RIDGE BOOK 3

ALISON STONE

TREEHAVEN PRESS

CHAPTER 1

*B*eefy fingers dug into Hannah Shetler's shoulder. Goose bumps raced up her bare arms. She froze in the ring of light that had captured her attempted escape. Her long hair fell in a curtain over her face, a strange sensation considering she had spent a lifetime wearing a tight bun hidden under a *kapp*. It felt even stranger to have a man touch her. Hold her painfully in place. Tuck a strand behind her ear, letting his rough knuckles brush across her cheek, the gentle gesture as painful as a slap.

Hannah gritted her teeth to keep them from chattering. She had witnessed his temper with the other girl in the house. The one who eyed Hannah with a wary gaze as if she were the competition. He seemed to get pleasure from other people's pain, their fear. Somewhere deep within, Hannah mustered the strength to hide hers. She refused to give him the satisfaction.

"Going out?" he asked in an amused tone, his stale breath whispering across her exposed neck.

Hannah lifted her chin and met his shadowed gaze. They

were alone except for the incessant chirp of the crickets. She cleared her throat. "I needed air."

He narrowed his eyes and hiked his chin to search beyond where she stood. "In the middle of the night?"

Nerves fluttered in Hannah's belly. A fit of quiet anger boiled just below the surface. She swallowed hard. "Yes, sir." The sign of respect clawed out of her throat.

"Bad things happen to solitary girls, especially in the dark." He grabbed a fistful of her hair and dragged her toward the door. His strength and the suddenness of the movement made her yelp.

"I'm sorry. I didn't—"

"Do you think I'm stu–pid?" he spit out the word in two distinct syllables like the boy in her single-room Amish school-house who struggled to read despite being one of the oldest. A plow horse had kicked him in the head. At least that's what her *dat* claimed when Timothy, her brother, made fun of him.

There but for the grace of Gott...

She shook away the image of her *dat*.

"Neh." The Amish word slipped out. "I needed air. Truly." The lie sprang from her lips but missed its mark. Instinctively, her arms flung to protect her scalp as he tightened his grip and ripped a clump of hair from its roots. A traitorous grunt tumbled from her lips.

"You Amish girls pretend to be all prissy." He leaned in close and licked her cheek. Her stomach heaved at the wet roughness of his tongue and the vileness of the act. She froze, her heart jackhammering in her chest.

She had been the stupid one. Without knowing the first thing about him she had accepted his invitation to work for his family. He claimed he and his father needed someone to clean their house. Prepare meals. She had thought it was an answer to her prayers. A job in Hunters Ridge while she figured out her future plans. Instead, she discovered an absent father and a waif of a girl who flinched every time he asked her to do chores. Immediately, she had realized her mistake, but had to bide her time to leave.

"You shouldn't have left the farm if you can't play with the big boys." He forced her up the steps of the front porch by her hair. She slowly blinked, lamenting her failed escape attempt.

But if she had, where would she have gone?

A cold dread coiled its way up her spine. Had her quiet roommate betrayed Hannah to their captor?

He opened the door and shoved her inside. Her shoulder slammed into the wall, but she remained on her feet. Her entire scalp ached from the assault, but she didn't dare move. He was liable to wrap a long strand around his fist and force her to the ground.

A jangle from the other room grew closer, accompanied by the clack of claws on the hardwood floor. He gave the dog a quick pat on the head. More perfunctory than affectionate. "Everything's okay, boy." She had never heard him call the dog by name.

The dog's eyes drifted from his master to Hannah. The dog didn't look convinced. He walked in tight circles, chasing his tail, then laid down and licked his paws.

"Right? You're going to be a good boy?" He nudged the dog with the toe of his boot. The dog gave him a deep guttural growl but didn't get up.

The man turned toward her. "How about you? You gonna be good?"

Hannah nodded, her heart racing. The stagnant air pressed on her, making her feel claustrophobic. She wished she had stayed in bed.

No...

She wished she had never left her family home in the first place.

Her worst day on the farm was glorious compared to the nightmare here.

"I want to go home." Hannah steeled her voice, trying to sound calm. Assertive. A woman with nothing to lose.

A slow smile crawled up his smug face and sparked a dancing menace in his eyes and a new flame of fear in her chest. Maybe she should have kept her mouth shut.

"You don't really want to go home. There's nothing there for you. Remember?"

Unease prickled her aching scalp. In her efforts to escape the tedium of caring for her *dat* and brothers, she had found herself in a far worse predicament. This was her punishment. This wasn't freedom.

The dog whined, sensing her distress. The man leaned down and roughly grabbed the dog's collar. "Get!" When the dog didn't move fast enough, the man raised his voice. "Go on now! Get!"

The dog jerked up onto all fours and seemed to struggle to find his footing on the hardwood floors. He lumbered down the hall with his head hanging low. Hannah understood the feeling. She'd never escape now. She had squandered the element of surprise.

"You, too," he yelled at Hannah.

She ran up the stairs with the man on her heels and a deepening dread twisting in her gut.

When she opened the bedroom door, the man gave her a parting grumble, "Ungrateful brats." Hannah closed the door behind her, relieved to be alone. A scraping sounded at the handle. She tried it.

Her stomach plummeted. He had locked her in. A first. She had wasted what was surely her one shot at freedom.

She backed away from the door. A shadow darkened the crack beneath.

"Tomorrow I'm taking you somewhere safe," the man said through the hollow door.

Safe? What did he mean? The words and the tears were silent. The walls closed in on her. She sank into the mattress and the hard wood frame cut into her thigh. An acute sense of being watched made her skin itch. Hannah shifted her body. Moonlight caught the wide, unblinking eyes of her roommate.

"You shouldn't have done that." The girl showed no emotion before she rolled over and covered her cheek with the rough sheet. Leaving only the top of her dark hair visible on the dingy white pillowcase.

"I was going to get help," Hannah whispered.

"I never asked for help." The pillow muffled her soft voice.

"Don't you want to go home?"

The girl groaned. Hannah couldn't be sure, but she thought she heard her roommate say, "So much worse."

Hannah let out a long breath and lay down on top of the covers, still dressed in her *Englisch* getaway clothes. She stared at the ceiling. The swaying branches cast shadows on the walls. She listened to the strange noises in the unfamiliar house. Her mind drifted to her bed at home.

Oh, what she wouldn't do to be home.

God was punishing her for disrespecting the *Ordnung*. Tears burned the back of her nose. The old Hannah would have been quick to accept her fate. To be the obedient daughter.

But this man wasn't her father.

And she wasn't the old Hannah.

His parting words haunted her as she drifted in and out of sleep. The sound of a key scraping in the lock made her bolt upright. The first signs of dawn softened the shadows in the room.

He's back.

He's back.

He's back.

Her fight-and-flight response kicked in on a rush of adrenaline. Her eyes darted around the room. She had nowhere to go. Absolutely nowhere.

The story of her life.

CHAPTER 2

$\mathcal{T}$he automatic doors on Hunters Ridge's one and only grocery store whooshed open and the heat from the asphalt parking lot warmed Sarah James's face. She missed Wegman's from her college days in Buffalo, but giving up her favorite grocery store was a small price to pay for being able to be here for Gramps. She owed him that much. She owed him far more than that. He had saved her when she was sixteen by allowing her to leave her parents' house when she was what her father would call "a teenager with oppositional defiance disorder." It must have been a term he heard in court or at the station. Nothing like the pot calling the kettle black. Sarah would call it "a sixteen-year-old trying to escape her father's iron fist."

Tomato. To-*ma*-to.

Sarah returned to Buffalo when it was time for college, and after she graduated she came back to Hunters Ridge to stay with Gramps. He wasn't getting any younger. And by returning, she had found a calling of sorts in this quaint, mostly Amish town. Her degree in social work came in handy after all.

A soft wind blew her hair from her face as she pushed the grocery cart to the return stall, the front right wheel squeaking and wobbling. The late afternoon sun reflected in the large puddles from an early morning storm. She grabbed the handles of the reusable grocery bag and hoisted it out of the cart. She'd spun around to head to her car when a woman dressed in a skirt that hung to mid-calf caught her eye.

Sarah smiled brightly. "Well hello, Annie." The elderly woman with silver hair and a beautiful complexion had long ago insisted on being called by her first name. Annie grew up in an Amish home and currently helped women like her former self to find transitional homes when they chose to leave the Amish. Annie hadn't gone far. She'd made a home among the *Englisch* right here in Hunters Ridge.

Their paths crossed because Sarah's work also brought her into contact with unhappy women who wanted to jump the fence, as the Amish called it. It was Sarah's calling: helping women out of situations where they felt trapped. The nature of her work called for discretion and secrecy, yet the women who needed her most found their way to her. At least some of them did.

"Hi, Sarah." Annie set her oversize purse in the seat of the cart Sarah had just abandoned. The clear plastic frames sitting on her nose were out of fashion a decade ago but worked on the sweet woman's heart-shaped face. "How's Hannah doing?"

Sarah slid the handles of the grocery bag up to the crook of her arm to ease the pressure in her palm. "Hannah?" she whispered and glanced around to make sure they were alone, then she took a step closer and repeated, "Hannah Shetler?"

"Yes." The first blush of concern colored the older woman's cheeks.

"I don't know. I haven't seen her in a long time. Not since before she left the Amish." Sarah scratched her forehead. "I gave Hannah your name, but I didn't realize she contacted you."

Sarah looked over her shoulder. They weren't smuggling drugs or doing anything illegal, but their mission wasn't what the Amish community would call *Gott's* work. Sarah imagined more than one Amish mother wished God would strike her dead. If the Amish were a vengeful type, which they claimed they weren't. One of their tenets was forgiveness...until one of their own went against the *Ordnung.* Then, they withheld their forgiveness and shunned the wayward son or daughter until they realized the error of their ways or could no longer stand being out in the cold.

Again, tomato, to-*ma*-to.

"Hannah stayed at my place after she decided she wanted to come home."

"She was returning home?" Sarah's heart stuttered. "Why did she leave a letter stating that she wanted to leave and live among the *Englisch*?"

"Yes, yes..." Annie's voice cracked, the unmistakable sound of aging. "I had heard rumblings, but you know, my George has been sick."

"I'm sorry. I'll keep him in my prayers." Sarah supposed the empty offer—she couldn't remember the last time she had prayed—would bring the elderly woman comfort.

Annie acknowledged her with a slight nod. "I'm getting forgetful." The corners of her pale lips curved downward. "Hannah showed up at my place and asked if she could stay a few days. I gave her a room, and she did stay, but she left sooner than I had expected. I suppose she felt unwelcomed. My house isn't exactly cozy with George's hospital bed in the middle of the family room."

Sarah touched the woman's hand resting on the handle of the grocery cart. "You've done so much to help these girls. You have no reason to be hard on yourself."

"*Yah*, well…" Annie looked away.

Sarah squeezed her hand. "I don't want to keep you from running your errands, but are you sure Hannah said she was going home? To her family's farm?" A ticking started in Sarah's brain.

"Yes, she called Chester for a ride." Chester Gilmore provided rides for the Amish since they weren't allowed to drive.

"When was this?" Sarah slowly dragged her hand through her hair, growing warm from the heat of the late afternoon sun.

"A few days ago?" A line creased her brow. "All the days blend with doctor's appointments and such. I didn't want to pry, but it's not unusual for a young woman to realize the choice she had been so eager to make wasn't for her, after all. The outside world is much different than the insular life of the Amish."

"It's an adjustment, that's for sure." Sarah set the grocery bag on the asphalt and the glass jars clanked as they shifted. She swiped the back of her hand across her forehead. "It's just that I haven't seen Hannah around town."

Annie braced her forearm on the handle of the grocery cart. "It seems strange, doesn't it? I hope she's not in any trouble."

"Perhaps she's staying close to the family farm." Sarah touched Annie's arm again. "She'll want to make her way back into their good graces. Someone who's looking to be forgiven wouldn't exactly have me on speed dial."

"That's for sure. Amish and speed dial." Annie giggled softly, appreciating Sarah's effort at levity. "I'm sure you're right. I worry about these young women. I remember being that age and struggling." A weariness replaced the spark in Annie's eyes. "It's hard to stay separate and not be tempted by the bigger world. I'm not sure what I would have done if I hadn't met my George."

"Sometimes I think it would be easier to hole up in a farm somewhere." Sarah scooped up the bags again.

"Minus the work. Oh, how I hated all the chores on the farm. They were never-ending." Annie laughed softly, but it lacked mirth.

"I can only imagine."

"Well, I better get moving. George will be looking for me." Annie took a couple steps, the shopping cart resuming its merry squeaking and wobbling, and now a high-pitched squeal joined the chorus. "Nice to see you, Sarah."

"You too, Annie."

Sarah popped the trunk and set the bag inside. Indecision made her nerves hum. She had been *so* looking forward to curling up with a tub of cookies-and-cream ice cream and her newest obsession on Netflix. Not anymore. She'd never relax until she knew Hannah was safe.

Sarah dropped the groceries off at the small apartment above the hardware store where she lived with Gramps. When she poked her head into the store from the office off the alley entrance, he was fiddling with something—like always—behind the counter.

His passion was the hardware store, the same one his father managed before him. He had the right amount of alone time to pursue his handyman projects, interrupted by the occasional customer to give him the socialization he craved. And he had the financial means to keep this place open. Or so Sarah hoped. Gramps was a private man, and he had the mental acuity to keep it that way. Sarah's name was on all the accounts, but Gramps made her promise to keep her nose out of them until he was six feet under.

Sarah's mother had no interest in the shop—or the town —where she was raised, leaving Hunters Ridge for college in Buffalo where she met and married Sarah's dad, a police officer. If Sarah and her father hadn't clashed, she might have never gotten to know her grandfather at all.

Sometimes good things came out of bad.

After a quick hello, Sarah hopped back into her car parked in the alley and made her way toward Route 76 and the Shetlers' farm. With any luck, she'd find Hannah at the vegetable stand by the road, the same one where Hannah's little brothers had claimed they last saw her before she finally got up the nerve to leave.

Sarah had found herself willing the most favorable outcome—complete with her on the couch with a spoon in one hand and the remote in the other—when she crested the hill near the Shetlers' farm. She slowed, debating if she should stick her nose some place it didn't belong. Because once she knew for sure that Hannah wasn't on the farm, she'd never find peace until she found her.

Please be here. Please be here.

Movement around the vegetable stand made Sarah's heart flutter with hope. She pulled her car along the berm of the road.

Please be here. Please be here.

A soft breeze rustled the corn stalks which would be ground up for feed soon. Sarah never lived on a farm, but living in Hunters Ridge for the better part of a decade had provided her with vicarious knowledge of their workings. She liked the cyclical nature of being tied to the land, even if she observed it from a distance. She might think differently if she had to get dirt under her nails.

Two young Amish boys kicked around a volleyball as if it

were a soccer ball. Hannah's twin brothers. If she remembered correctly, they couldn't be more than ten or so. One of the boys pivoted to stop the ball with the toe of his dusty boot like a well-trained soccer player. His eyes tracked her movements as she climbed out of the car and waved.

"Hello there." She crossed the uneven ground, careful to avoid the puddles. She held her breath, fearing the boys would alert their father. The boy's face crunched up with concern. Perhaps she had played this all wrong.

She shifted her gaze toward the wooden vegetable stand. An Amish woman stood with her back to her while organizing the corn into neat piles. Relief played at the edges of her mind.

Ice cream, here I come.

"Hannah…"

The woman slowly turned around. The start of a smile disappeared from the young Amish woman's face. "I'm…"

"Emma Mae," Sarah finished. Hannah's brother's fiancée. "How are you?" The forced cheeriness made her simple question sound strained.

"Gut." Emma Mae glanced over her shoulder toward the house, the string of her bonnet draping over her shoulder. Her stiff posture suggested she wasn't up for small talk. Or maybe it was Sarah she wasn't up for. "Can I help you?"

"I'm looking for Hannah."

One of the boys tucked the ball under his arm and approached the vegetable stand. His curious round eyes grew narrow. "My sister moved away."

"What's your name?" Sarah asked.

"Joseph. My brother's Jacob." She imagined the square-shouldered boy was the spokesman of the youngest Shetler duo.

"Hi, Joseph. My name's Sarah. I'm a friend of Hannah's." Was she really? More like a professional acquaintance. "Has your sister stopped by the house recently?" Sarah softened her tone and bent at the waist to better see the boy's eyes under his broad-brimmed hat.

"*Neh*, she's gone for *gut*." Sadness glistened in his shadowed gaze. "Our neighbor looked for her and everything. She's in law enforcement." His lower lip trembled. "Told us Hannah left on her own to live with the *Englischers*."

Emma Mae flicked her fingers at Joseph, not bothering to hide her annoyance with the heartbroken kid. "Go on, now. Adults are talking."

The boy studied Sarah for a second, then dropped the ball and gave it a solid kick. His brother chased it into the cornfield.

"We don't talk about Hannah." Emma Mae gave Sarah a cold, hard stare. "The corn is fresh. Six cobs for a dollar." The Amish woman tried to strike a look of indifference, but Sarah noted the hard edges.

"I'm not interested in corn."

A deep line marred Emma Mae's face. "Joseph told you. Hannah left." She lowered her voice. "You helped her leave." Sarah figured Emma Mae's accusatory glare was a reflex. "So why are you trying to stir things up?"

"That's not my intention. I need to know she's safe."

"She made her choice," Emma Mae said and hiked her chin.

Anger bubbled just below the surface. "We all get to make choices." Sarah's gaze dropped to Emma Mae's waist. Rumors traveled fast in a small town. But this was one Emma Mae and Timothy, Hannah's brother, hoped to keep secret. "When are you getting married?"

Emma Mae had the good sense to lower her eyes and blush. "In two weeks." Did the young Amish woman realize she was cradling her midsection? "Hannah has been a *gut* friend." She lowered her voice to barely a whisper and her words turned wistful. "She took blame for the suitcase Mr. Shetler found in the barn before Timothy and I changed our minds and decided we'd stay. Raise our children Amish." She rubbed her lips together and glanced nervously toward the house. "I promise you, I haven't seen Hannah since she left. She wouldn't want you causing trouble now that everything's settled." She lifted her timid eyes. "Let things be."

Sarah studied the young Amish woman. She couldn't be more than eighteen and yet she was pregnant and getting married. The Amish would have preferred to reverse the order, but people were people, with or without plain clothing.

Sarah scratched her neck. It was buggy out here. "I'm a social worker. I help people. And I'm worried about Hannah. A friend of mine said she planned to return home."

Alarm lit Emma Mae's eyes. "Here?"

"Yes, but I'm not one hundred percent certain I just need to make sure she's okay."

Emma Mae fidgeted with the stacks of corn, lining the cobs up in neat rows. "I haven't seen her. It wonders me if this person was confused." She shrugged, the casual gesture at odds with the stiff set of her body. "She hasn't been here."

Then why did Annie think Hannah had gone home? Maybe Hannah lied to Annie. But why? Sarah swatted at a mosquito while canvassing the surrounding farm. Hannah'd have no reason to lie. Not to Annie.

"You need to leave," Emma Mae said, a brittleness in her voice. "Her brothers really miss their big sister. It's not right for you to come here and raise their expectations. This is supposed to be a happy time with my wedding and all."

"I..." Sarah shook her head. This was an argument she wasn't going to win.

The crash of the screen door made them both spin around. Mr. Shetler stood on the front porch. His long, unkempt beard reached halfway down his chest. "Jacob! Joseph! Come," he bellowed.

Emma Mae turned toward Sarah. "Go. Now."

The mixture of fear and panic on Emma Mae's face reminded Sarah of how she had felt when her father arrived home from his shift at the police department. He'd always be tired and angry and ready to take it out on whoever got in his way. Sarah did her best to make sure she wasn't the one in the way, but as a child, that wasn't always possible. And her mother had been as docile as the Amish girls she called friends during her teenage years in Hunters Ridge.

Some of whom Sarah later helped leave Hunters Ridge and the Amish community.

Sarah shook her head, dismissing the memory. She gave Emma Mae a quick nod, eager to let the young woman off the hook. She didn't have a police officer for a father, but her grandfather was the bishop. If anyone found out about her pregnancy, it would cast shame not only on her family, but the head of their Amish district.

"I'm going." Sarah took a step backward. "If you see Hannah, *please* tell her to stop by the hardware store. I'd like to talk to her."

If Sarah hadn't been watching the Amish woman, she would have missed the slight nod of her head.

"Congratulations on your wedding."

"Denki." Thank you. Emma Mae's tone grew more urgent. "You need to go."

CHAPTER 3

*O*ondering if she was wasting her time, Sarah had pulled away from the Shetlers' cornfield when she caught sight of Deputy Olivia Cooper's home. The deputy and Hannah had become friends of sorts since they lived next door to each other. Sarah made a quick decision to pull into the deputy's driveway. The pickup truck parked out front buoyed her hopes that she was home.

Sarah crossed her fingers that Olivia would tell her, "Oh, of course I've seen Hannah. She's been home for weeks. Haven't you heard? I'm not sure why Timothy's fiancée told you otherwise."

Sarah had climbed the porch of the neat little bungalow and lifted her fist to knock when the door flew open. Startled, she took a step backward, surprised to find a handsome man standing in the doorway with car keys at the ready. Her hand flew to her chest. "Oh, I'm sorry." Her first instinct was to assume she had the wrong house. "I was looking for—"

"Olivia?" A crooked smile tilted half his mouth. "You've got the right place."

"Oh good."

"Come on in." Even though Sarah had lived in Hunters Ridge since the age of sixteen, she still couldn't get over the friendliness—the openness—of a small town. Growing up in Buffalo, she wouldn't welcome a stranger into her home. Her father, the police officer, had shared too many horror stories. He even had a camera on his front door so he could see who was there without taking his eyes off his seventy-inch TV screen.

"Olivia, you have company." The man held out his hand. "I'm sorry. I didn't catch your name. Drew Kincaid." After they shook hands, he jerked his thumb toward Olivia who was sitting on the couch with a blanket over her lap. "I stopped by to make sure she had everything she needed."

"Um…" Sarah glanced around, confused, unsure of what was going on. "…I'm Sarah James. My grandpa owns the hardware store in town."

Drew's eyes lit up. "Of course. Russ. Good guy. He told me about you. Pleasure to meet you."

"Yeah, you too. I mostly stick to the office in back. Gramps loves to chat with the customers."

"Lots of paperwork, huh?" Drew lifted a questioning eyebrow, but she suspected the question was more out of politeness than genuine curiosity.

"The usual business paperwork, but I'm also a social worker. I see clients in back, too." Sarah wasn't sure why she was rambling. Maybe to explain why someone who frequented the store hadn't met her.

"Well…" He walked over and kissed the top of Olivia's head and gently patted her arm. Sarah's heart melted at the display of affection. "If you're all set, I'm going to get back to the lumberyard."

"Thanks, honey," Olivia said. "I'm good."

Sarah watched Drew leave, and once the door clicked shut she turned to Olivia. "Are you okay?" She tilted her head and frowned.

Olivia smiled, leaned forward, grabbed a corner of the blanket covering her legs and tossed it back revealing a cast. "Busted my ankle. Chasing a drunk Amish kid who bailed on his wagon." She grimaced in disgust. "I leapt over a ditch and landed wrong. But I caught him. By the hem of his pants. Kid decided getting arrested would be smarter than showing up without his pants." She laughed. "How do you supposed he'd explain that to his parents?"

"Ugh. Sorry about that."

"Hazard of the job. The sheriff promised he'd put me on desk duty next week. I might go stir-crazy before then." She scratched her forehead. "A person can only stream so many shows, you know?"

"Yeah."

Olivia shrugged, tucked the blanket back in around her legs and then lowered the volume on a flat-screen TV that dominated the opposite wall. "What brings you my way? Don't tell me another Amish girl has gone missing." Her tone was light, but the message had dark underpinnings.

Technically, the young Amish women Sarah helped to leave Hunters Ridge *wanted* to go missing, but Sarah's cheeks grew warm with the subtle admonition all the same. She drew in a deep breath and let it out, feeling like she was on a cliff ready to be pushed off. "No, not another girl. The same one."

Olivia stiffened her back and braced her right hand on the cushion next to her. She winced, then collapsed into the softness of the couch. "You have to be kidding me."

"You've seen Hannah, then?"

"No. Not recently. Correct me if I'm wrong, but I thought

we resolved this weeks ago. She left a note saying she had left Hunters Ridge. I recognized the handwriting from previous notes from her."

Sarah relayed her conversation with Annie about Hannah calling for a ride home.

A look of frustration swept across Olivia's face. "I wish I wasn't laid up." She pressed her lips together. "Do you think she lied to Annie about her plans?"

"It's possible. But I can't shake this bad feeling."

"Yeah, I don't like the sound of it, either." Olivia grabbed a wooden back scratcher from the coffee table. She slid the handle end in the narrow space between her cast and leg and jimmied it back and forth vigorously while clenching her teeth and rolling her eyes back. "I'm so itchy."

Sarah smiled. She couldn't help herself. She had never broken a bone. *Knock on wood.* "Any ideas where Hannah might go?" They had been through all this before. A young woman who lived her whole life on a farm in Hunters Ridge wouldn't exactly have places she haunted outside of that same small town.

"I'll make a few phone calls, but I doubt the sheriff's department will take this on. We're short on staff as it is, even before I busted my ankle."

"But Annie Yutzy—"

Olivia tossed the back scratcher, and it landed with a thwack on the couch. "From everything we've uncovered, Hannah has been very coy about leaving Hunters Ridge. Perhaps she was lying to Annie." Olivia blew out a long breath. "I hate it that the Amish culture forced Hannah to be secretive and now we don't know if she's in danger."

"I can do a little follow-up. I have the name of the driver Annie said she called. I'll track him down. He can tell us where he took her." Sarah cleared her throat.

Olivia leaned forward, as if she wanted to get up.

Sarah held up her palm. "Take it easy or your boyfriend will hunt me down." She laughed, despite the anxiety swirling in her gut.

"Ah, Drew's a softie. Not sure what I did to deserve him."

Sarah raised a subtle eyebrow. She wouldn't know anything about that. After growing up under the iron fist of her father, she had no desire to get involved with a man, especially one inclined to keep her under his thumb. Independence was too appealing. But caring for someone was altogether different. Something stirred in her heart, but she ignored it. Life was simpler when she lived it on her own terms. No one to worry about but herself.

And the occasional Amish girl who went missing.

"Seems like a nice guy." Even though Sarah didn't care for conventional relationships, she had been brought up to be polite. Who was she to rain on someone else's parade?

"He is." Olivia wiggled her toes poking out at the top of the cast. She must have painted her nails pink before the accident. "Would you hand me my cell phone? It's on the edge of the coffee table."

Sarah handed it to her.

"Thanks." She slid her finger across the screen. "Give me your cell phone number. I'll contact you if I hear anything."

"That would be great."

"You do the same, please?" Olivia smiled. "Hannah and I were fairly close. She'd come over and visit quite often." She made a sound with her lips closed. "Sometimes I wonder if I unknowingly gave her the idea to leave. She probably envied my life." She shook her head. "Poor kid had to raise her younger brothers from the day they were born. Their mother died in childbirth."

"That's horrible. But don't be hard on yourself. I've

learned that you can't give someone ideas that weren't already in their head." This was how Sarah justified helping Amish women leave Hunters Ridge—she provided women with options.

"You're right. I'd be rich if I had a dime for every person who told me it wasn't their idea to spray paint on the bridge or smash the windows in the used car lot or spin their tires in the empty fields…" Olivia drew a small circle in the air, suggesting she could go on and on. Her soft giggle indicated an easygoing manner. Perhaps Sarah should reach out to the young deputy when it didn't involve Hannah. She could use a few friends.

"Can I do anything for you before I leave?" Sarah asked.

Olivia lifted the remote and pointed it at the TV without turning up the volume. "I can entertain myself for a few hours. Thanks."

Sarah nodded and then let herself out. She sidestepped the water that had gathered in the ruts from the earlier rain. The cornstalks fluttered in the wind. For a fraction of a second, she thought she saw something dark darting in and out in between the rows of corn.

Heart racing, she stopped and approached the edge of the field. "Hello?" A chill coursed down her spine and the urge to run nearly overwhelmed her. She blew out a hard breath, calming her nerves. There were still a few hours of daylight. No reason to freak out. "Hello? Is someone there?"

The papery rustling of wind blowing through the stalks was the only reply. She squinted in the direction of the movement. After a moment, she chalked it up to her imagination—or perhaps one of the Shetler boys chasing their ball —but she hustled to her car all the same. Sometimes she wondered why she got involved with things that made her have to double-check the locks on her doors and question her sanity for caring.

But she remembered why. A few tragic events illuminated the hopelessness created by limited choices. By being trapped.

She snapped the seat belt buckle into place and squared her shoulders in determination. She had to find Hannah. Make sure she was still in control of her comings and goings.

The alternative was too scary to contemplate.

Sarah grabbed her cell phone and dialed the number of the car service that Annie had said Hannah used. It went directly to what sounded like an old-fashioned answering machine. Unless Chester Gilmore forgot to update the outgoing message, he was out of town visiting a sick relative.

She was about to toss her phone into her purse when it rang. Gramps's smiling face popped up on the screen. Her mood automatically lifted.

"Hey, Gramps."

"Hello, there." He seemed to be making an extra effort to sound cheery, but she had learned a long time ago to stop asking him if he was okay because the answer would always be the same. "Are you on your way home?"

"Um, is something up?"

"I was hoping you could work the register this afternoon so I could catch the game."

"Game?"

"Baseball."

"Yeah, sure." Sarah could have sworn he was watching a football game yesterday. She hoped he didn't detect the hesitation in her voice. Gramps was a baseball fan, but he usually put the game on the TV near the register. He must be tired. "Be home in ten minutes."

"Sounds good." He sighed. "I don't know what I'd do without you."

"Love you."

"Love you too, Sarah."

She tossed her phone on the passenger seat and then put the car into Drive. She'd have to put her plans on hold.

CHAPTER 4

*S*pecial Agent Trevor Griffin sat at his desk at the Buffalo Field Office of the FBI. The neat columns of numbers on his computer screen had grown wavy, and he blinked in a failed attempt to make the lines straight again. He scrubbed his face. The people who heard "FBI agent" and thought "badge, gun, and catching the bad guy" were often let down when he explained that he spent most of his days in front of spreadsheets as part of the white-collar crime unit.

Bor-ring. Why did they always drag out the word?

Boring caught the bad guy. Following the money often led him down a path to the bad guy. It wasn't glamorous, but it was effective.

And it was his job.

Griff, his nickname since he played high school JV football, rolled his neck, trying to ease out the kinks. His gaze flicked to the corner of his laptop screen. Almost quitting time. He didn't watch the clock by nature, but today had been a long day. He pressed his thumbs into his temples, hoping to stem the subtle ache pulsing behind his eyes.

Griff's cell phone vibrated on the glass surface of his desk.

His sister's smiling face appeared on the screen. The photo had been taken at her engagement party. He really needed to swap that image out, especially since she was in the middle of a contentious divorce.

He slid his finger across the smartphone's screen. "Hey, Jeannie."

"Hey, Griff." He detected concern in the short greeting.

"What's wrong? Mom okay?" Their elderly mother was part of the reason he stuck to the relative safety of the white-collar crime unit.

"Mom?" His sister seemed to be thrown off by the simple question. "Mom? Um, yes. Mom's fine. I guess. I haven't talked to her today, but we went to church yesterday. So, yeah, she's fine." A suspense-filled pause stretched across the line. "It's Lexi."

"Lexi?" His eighteen-year-old niece had been pushing the boundaries since she was fifteen, which just so happened to coincide with the first time her mother caught her father cheating. It had been three years of arguing, culminating in the current divorce battle. "Is she okay?"

"That's the thing. I don't know. She left the house Saturday afternoon and she hasn't come home." The quiver in her voice was unmistakable.

"Saturday?" He looked at his watch, as if that would confirm what he already knew. "Two days ago?" He pushed away from his desk and stood. "Did you call the police? Tell me you called the police." Griff loved his sister, but he didn't always agree with her decisions. Point in case: her choice in a husband. But in the end, the guy had given his sister three beautiful daughters, including Lexi. Wild, devil-may-care Lexi.

Jeannie's voice grew soft. "I can't. She's done this twice before. It usually has to do with a boy…" Griff envisioned his sister vigorously rubbing her forehead, her glasses sliding down her nose. "She always comes back, but she's never been gone for more than one night."

Lexi had mastered the art of seeking attention, but what if she had gotten into real trouble this time? "Is there a new guy?"

"Not that she's shared with me. I tried getting on her laptop, but it's password protected. Her social media sites are all locked down, too. But she forgot one thing. I tracked her phone."

Good job, sis.

"She's eighteen," Jeannie said, her voice sounding distant. "I figured the police would tell me she's an adult and can come and go as she pleases."

"Where did you track her to?"

"That's what has me worried. She spent Friday night at her best friend's house. She stopped home for a change of clothes and left again without telling me where she was going. The app showed that she headed into Jamestown on Saturday. I tracked the phone to some place out in the country. A town called Hunters Ridge."

Griff sat down, grabbed the edge of his desk, and rolled up under the keyboard. He opened a map website and entered the name Hunters Ridge. "That's about an hour from here." His mind raced. "Did you try calling her?" No question was too obvious during the initial stages of an investigation. Was that what this was? He ran a hand across his mouth.

"Called. Texted. Left voicemails. No response." Jeannie muttered something under her breath. "A few hours ago, I lost contact with the phone."

"Maybe she lost charge?"

"Have you ever known a teenager not to find a charger?"

Griff shrugged, even though his sister couldn't see him. "What are you thinking?"

"I think Lexi's in trouble." Oddly, his sister's tone sounded more exhausted than concerned. Or maybe the flat affect spoke more of defeat.

Griff's stomach sank. The world was a dangerous place. "Do you have an exact address?"

"I have the general area. I can take a screenshot and send it to you."

"You want me to check it out?"

"Yes, I'd do it myself—"

"No, you were smart to call me. You shouldn't go to a strange place by yourself." He reached over and powered down his laptop. "I'm headed out of the office now."

"Thank you." The words rushed out on a sigh of relief. "I have to get Lulu and Mimi to gymnastics. With everything else, I hate to mess with their routine."

"How's it going?" *It* being the divorce.

His sister's laugh came out as a sharp bark. "Have you ever heard of someone having a good divorce?"

"True." His soon-to-be former brother-in-law's big mug floated into his mind. He was hard to deal with on a good day.

"Nate's fighting me for custody of the girls." The girls being Lexi's younger sisters, Lulu and Mimi. Lexi was technically an adult.

"You're kidding me." The guy hardly spent any time with his children when they lived under the same roof. Griff had subbed in more times than he could count when it came to father-related events at school. Good old Uncle Griff. He never minded. It was his pleasure. Nate didn't seem to realize what he was missing...

"Ever since I lost my job and my lawyer drew up papers that stated Nate had to increase child support, he wants custody of the girls. Pure retaliation. The jerk... That's why I'm afraid to call the police. This could be another one of

Lexi's stunts. It'll give him just the ammunition he needs to take the girls."

"Do you really think it's a stunt?"

"It has to be, right?" His sister's voice cracked, then grew soft as if she were afraid someone would overhear. "I need to make sure she's okay." She cleared her throat. "She's my baby girl."

Griff stood and slipped on his suit coat. "I'm leaving now." He glanced down at his phone, at the map his sister had sent him.

"Thanks, Griff. I can't thank you enough."

"What are families for?" He slammed the lid of his laptop closed and tucked in his chair. "Keep your phone close by. I'll call as soon as I get to Hunters Ridge. I'm sure she's fine."

Griff wasn't sure of anything. He had no idea what he'd find once he got to Hunters Ridge, but his need to protect his sister was strong, even though he was the younger brother. His father had always told him he'd be the man of the house if something were to happen to him.

And it had. A long time ago.

And Griff took his promises seriously.

A little over an hour later, Griff had arrived at the last known location of his niece's cell phone: Potter Road on the outskirts of Hunters Ridge, a small town in Western New York.

During the drive, he'd remained calm, figuring—hoping—Lexi was safe. She always seemed to come out unscathed from whatever adventures she set out on, much to the relief of the family who loved her tremendously. This time, she had probably run off to hang with her friends and to avoid the hassles of her mother and father's perpetual arguing over their divorce. His sister said the therapist claimed Lexi was looking for attention. Apparently in all the wrong places.

Poor kid.

Griff understood what it was like to grow up in a nontraditional home. His mother had to raise two children alone after her husband died of cancer. His father had been a Buffalo cop and his "brothers in blue" were like family. Dad's former coworkers had filled in where he never could. The tragedy had made Jeannie and Griff very close.

Now Jeannie struggled to care for three children and deal with a man who never grew up and refused to take responsibility. Apparently, the latest legal wrangling on her ex's part was meant to annoy—not proof that he was now manning up and was willing to do more than his share in child-rearing. Her ex wanted to put Jeannie through the wringer. Again.

Lexi's antics wouldn't help. Her dad would use it as evidence that his sister was ill-equipped to raise productive adults. The law might come down on her ex's side. They couldn't take that chance.

Griff tapped the brake, slowing to check the screenshot on his phone of Lexi's last known location. He looked up and blinked and exhaled sharply. It had been a really long day, and it didn't seem to be ending any time soon. A lonely house sat back among some trees. He drove past it, then made a U-turn and drove slowly toward the house again. It was the only house in sight. He turned up the driveway. The house sat in heavy shadows as the sun dipped lower in the sky. The closer he got, the more he realized it was in need of some TLC. His stomach pitched.

The house looked abandoned, a place that squatters and drug dealers would use if it were in the city. What in the world would Lexi's phone be doing here? As far as he knew, his niece courted trouble, but she hadn't gotten involved with drugs.

Has she?

Griff scrubbed his hand across his face. "Oh, Lexi," he muttered. His latest FBI case had kept him very busy. Too busy to do his regular check-ins with his nieces. How long had it been? The afternoon coffee that he knew he shouldn't have had made his stomach turn sour.

He undid his tie and slid it out from around his neck. He loosened the top couple buttons, hoping to not look every bit the FBI agent that he was. He debated taking off his suit coat, but he needed to conceal the gun holstered underneath. He had no idea what he was walking into.

He pushed open the car door and stepped out. The heat from earlier in the day had begun to dissipate. The forecast on morning radio called for more showers rolling into the area. He glanced around, taking in the house and surrounding property. A detached garage had a busted window, and farther back among the trees was a dilapidated barn. Based on the barren land, he doubted any farming had gone on here in the recent past. Was it an Amish home? He didn't see any horses or buggies or washing on the line.

Not even a car.

Griff walked the perimeter of the house. The place seemed deserted. He climbed the front steps and knocked on the door. No answer.

He stepped off the porch and strode around back. The tall grass came as no surprise. He wished he had something more casual than his shiny dress shoes. His gaze tracked to the abandoned barn. Since he was here, why not check it out? He didn't have a warrant, but he wasn't here on official business. He'd just take a peek. The soft earth squished around his shoes. Better to ask for forgiveness than permission.

He had taken a few steps across the long field toward the barn when someone called to him.

"Yo, bro. You need something?"

So much for someone not being home.

Griff slowly turned around, half expecting to find a shotgun aimed at his chest. *Isn't that usually how these things go?* Inwardly he rolled his eyes. He had been sitting behind a desk for far too long. But thankfully, the man didn't have a gun and Griff wouldn't have to explain to his boss why he had been gunned down by some farmer while he was worried about getting his shoes muddy. Griff would have been a cautionary tale for generations of FBI agents to come.

Griff relaxed his shoulders and stuffed his hands into his pants pocket, trying to appear casual despite wearing a business suit in the middle of a field in the middle of nowhere. "Yes, I do need something." He took a step toward the man. A kid almost. Barely out of his teens.

"Are you law enforcement?" the kid asked.

Griff dodged the question by saying, "I'm looking for my niece. She's been missing since Saturday. Her name's Lexi. Alexis Camp. Pretty. Long dark hair."

The man's face fell momentarily before he seemed to catch himself. Or was Griff reading too much into it?

"Just me here." He waved his hand, gesturing for Griff to get out of his yard. He obliged and stepped back onto the gravel driveway. From where he stood, he couldn't see into the garage. The windows lined the top of the doors that swung on hinges. The structure must have been built halfway through the last century.

"Have you had company recently?" He studied the kid. "My niece is about your age. Maybe you had a party? Some girls you didn't know showed up?"

"Pfft, not likely. Have you seen this place? Not like I'd be inviting people I knew to come here. A guy's gotta have some pride." The kid scratched his head and his dark hair stood on edge. He wasn't exactly his niece's type. She tended to go for the tall, muscular, and athletic, not thin, unkempt, and ghostly white. He probably spent his days in front of a screen.

The kid shifted his weight from one foot to the other and his gaze darted around. "Is your niece from around here?"

Griff decided to be upfront with the kid. Gauge his reaction. "We're from the Buffalo area. I tracked her cell phone here."

The kid laughed. It sounded more strangled than humorous. "People leave all sorts of things in my dad's van."

"Your dad's van?" An image of a white van with the words *ICE CREAM* in do-it-yourself lettering sprang to mind. Surely Lexi wasn't that naïve.

The young man laughed again, a squeaky sound. "Not like it sounds. My dad drives the locals—a lot of Amish. He does pick up the occasional outsider."

"Outsider?" Griff felt his forehead furrow.

"People who aren't Amish."

Interesting.

"Come on in." Stubble made a scratching noise when the young man ran his hand along his jaw. "Let's see if I can find it from the items my dad cleared out of the van. He keeps a lost-and-found box in the house."

"I'd appreciate that." Griff followed him around to the front door. "I didn't catch your name."

The kid slowed on the front porch and gave him a once-over. "Nick Gilmore. People tend to call me Nicky."

"Seems like you have a real peaceful setup out here."

A muscle started ticking in Nick's jaw. "It's my dad's place. Chester. Most people know him. I'm just staying here till I save up a few bucks." He shrugged. Eager to get on with things, Nick unlocked the front door.

Had he locked it when he came out to confront him? Odd, considering there wasn't anyone else around.

Griff waited by the door as Nick hung a right into the

family room where an old TV perched precariously on a collapsible TV tray. The smell of old food and body sweat lingered in the closed-up space. The place could use a good airing out. Nicky rooted through a box, then held up his finger, as if there were more than one place to find lost items. A buzz hummed along Griff's nerve endings, his attention on high alert. This guy could pull out anything. He glanced up the stairs to the empty landing and made sure he maintained access to an exit. A way to escape.

Nicky shot him a furtive gaze, as if he wasn't used to company. He dragged out another box tucked behind a stack of books and whipped out a random glove, a snow scraper, a shoe—

Griff let out an audible breath.

Nick paused, his back stiffened, but he didn't turn around. "Hold on. Hold on." He shuffled to the other room. Griff remained by the front door. The kid reappeared a moment later, a sheepish expression on his pale face. "Is this what you're looking for?"

Griff's stomach dropped. He recognized Lexi's Hello Kitty cell phone case. But he had to be sure. He turned the phone over. The screen was blank. "Do you have a charger?"

A flicker of anger crossed the kid's face before he regained composure. "Yeah, man. In here." Nick led him farther into the house into what was most likely the original kitchen. It was filled with enough tchotchkes to rival the most committed hoarder. A charger was plugged into the wall. Nick held out his hand. "All yours."

"It should only take a minute." Griff plugged it in and waited. He studied his surroundings as discreetly as he could because Nick never took his eyes off him. His intuition told him this kid was hiding something dark. A creak sounded from overhead. "You here alone?" He drew comfort from the solidity of his holster hidden under his jacket.

Nick leaned against the edge of the small kitchen table and the legs skidded a few inches on the orange linoleum. He adjusted his weight and said, "Yeah. Me and my dog." He shrugged. "Old house makes a lot of settling noises."

Griff nodded, unconvinced. "Should be just another minute." He forced a smile and tapped on the black smartphone screen.

"Not like I don't have anything to do." Nick's tone suggested he was getting irritated.

Lexi's phone came to life with a familiar chime. The home screen indicated it was locked. He blew out a long breath of frustration. "Can you tell me where my niece was picked up?"

Nick shrugged. "No idea. Like I said, my dad collects all sorts of junk from his van. No telling when she was picked up."

"So, your dad took this fare? You didn't."

Nick's jaw twitched, and he gave a quick nod. "It's my dad's work. Not mine. He's out of town. When he's gone, they tend to call Peter. He's another taxi service in town. So it's been a little quiet around here."

"How can I reach your dad?" Griff asked, his BS detector sounding in his head.

"He's away visiting my sick aunt. He doesn't have a cell phone. He gets calls here on the landline." Nick handed Griff a simple business card with his dad's name and phone number.

"How long has he been gone?" Griff needed something. Once he left here, he'd have nothing to go on.

"Left yesterday. Not sure when he's coming back. My aunt's pretty sick." Nick stared at him, a flatness in his eyes that made Griff's blood run cold.

"Can I have your aunt's phone number? It's important."

"My aunt can barely pay for treatment, never mind a phone. Dad told me service got cut off last month. Sorry."

Nick peeled off the table and squared his shoulders. "Leave me your number. I'll have him call you as soon as he comes home."

A dog barked somewhere deep in the house. Upstairs, maybe.

"How do you get around?"

"I've got friends."

Griff studied him a moment before pulling out his wallet. He slid a business card across the surface of the table. If Nick was surprised by the FBI logo, he didn't show it. This kid had been all shuffling feet and dangling arms outside, but now he seemed calm. Devoid of emotion. As if he had flipped an emotional switch.

"Where do teenagers hang around in Hunters Ridge? Maybe I'll find her there."

He shrugged again. "There's a diner. Closest thing we have to a coffee shop." Nick scrubbed a hand across his hair, leaving it in messy tufts. "And if she's into...well, if she's into drugs, people hang out in the empty building next to the diner." His brows drew down. "Um...need directions?"

"I'll find it." Griff waited until the young man headed toward the front door. He didn't want to turn his back to him. When they reached the door Griff smiled, trying to disarm the man with a little charm. It rarely worked on guys. "Does your dad pick up passengers through one of the ride-sharing apps?" That was the only way his niece caught rides.

Nick arched a brow in disbelief. "Dude, my dad doesn't even have a smartphone." The young man's smile didn't reach his eyes. "Check out the diner. You're wasting your time here."

"I'll do that." Griff lifted his niece's phone. "And thanks for this."

As soon as Griff stepped outside, he drew in a deep breath. The small, dark house had made him feel claustrophobic. As he climbed into his truck, he scanned the property. He couldn't help but wonder what was in the garage and the barn, but even though he couldn't see Nick Gilmore, he sensed the kid was watching him from one of the windows. He'd bet a year's wages on it. Which meant he'd never get close to the outbuildings unless he had a warrant or came back when the kid wasn't around.

What did he have to hide?

Something was seriously off with that kid. He prayed his niece hadn't gotten tangled up with him.

CHAPTER 5

 couple hundred feet past the house on Potter Road, Griff pulled over on the gravel berm. He opened the GPS app on his phone and searched for Main Street, Hunters Ridge, NY. What appeared to be the center of the small town was only nine minutes away. It was after seven in the evening. Maybe he'd catch a few diners having a late dinner. He could show a photo of his niece around. See if anyone recognized her.

Maybe he'd get lucky.

But first he had to do something he was dreading. He hit Jeannie's number on his contact list and his sister answered immediately.

"Did you find her?" The hopeful anticipation in her breathless voice broke his heart.

"No, sorry." He held his breath and counted to three. "I found her phone."

"Oh no…" He could only imagine the scenario Jeannie was conjuring up. His niece's phone minus his niece. This was definitely not a good turn of events.

"No, no, it's not bad." He forced an encouraging tone,

trying to keep his sister off the ledge. "Lexi left her phone in a taxi." He didn't want to get into the specifics. It seemed too complicated—and unlikely—that his niece had somehow found a ride with a gentleman whose main clientele were the Amish. "I picked it up at the van owner's house."

"That doesn't sound right. Lexi would never leave her phone behind."

"Maybe it fell out of her bag and she didn't realize it."

"Not how these kids keep tabs on their phones. She would have realized it immediately and called…or texted or however they use those apps. That's what she used? One of those apps?"

He doesn't have a cell phone. He gets calls here on the landline. Nick's grating voice whispered across his brain and a sense of urgency had Griff drumming his fingers on the steering wheel. "That's all the information I have." Nothing good could come from getting his sister more freaked out than she already was. "We'll get to the bottom of it." He tried to sound more confident than he felt.

His sister's quiet sobs sounded over the line.

"Jeannie, we'll find her. Come on now…"

"I should have been a better parent. I was too preoccupied with the divorce. She always acted out to get my attention. What if—"

"Stop. This isn't your fault." In the rearview mirror, he absentmindedly watched a horse and buggy approach on the long country road. The rhythmic sound of the horse's hooves grew louder as it approached. Once it passed his parked vehicle, he noticed two Amish children hunkered down in the back of the buggy. The little boys stared out from under straw hats with an "I've seen it all" gaze. They must get tired of tourists gawking at them. He turned his attention to the screen in front of him. Precious seconds ticked by. "I'm going into town. See if I can find her. Hang tight."

Silence stretched over the phone line. He wished he could pull his big sister into an embrace like she did when they were kids. She had always reassured him that everything would be okay. Now it was his turn.

"I'll call you—" He put the gear into Drive but kept his foot on the brake.

"I should meet you in Hunters Ridge," Jeannie said, her voice urgent and high-pitched. "It's not far from Buffalo, right?" She sighed heavily, perhaps reasoning that her daughter couldn't have gone *that* far. "It'll be better if both of us are looking for her."

"No, you have the girls." Lexi's younger sisters were much younger. "Take care of them. Let me dig a little deeper. If Lexi doesn't show up in the next twenty-four hours, then we can talk about you joining me."

"Twenty-four hours?" His sister's tone bordered on hysteria, but he respected her too much to call her out on it.

"I'll find her. I promise."

"You've always kept your promises." She sniffed. "And Lexi always shows up." Her forced laugh lacked amusement. "Right?"

"Right."

"I've been praying, and I told God I wouldn't punish her if He'd just return her to me. Oh *please.*"

Griff didn't have any children and could only imagine his sister's pain and worry. "I love Lexi. I'll bring her home."

"Mmmhmm…" She seemed far away.

"I'll talk to you soon. And Jeannie…I love you."

"Love you, too."

Griff ended the call. Once back on the road, he easily caught up with the horse and buggy. The little boys riding in the back no longer seemed interested in him. They sat on a flat bed with their knees pulled up to their chests. He wondered how the Amish skirted New York State laws regarding seat belts and car seats and such. Dismissing the random thought, he waited until it was safe to pass. The Amish driver tipped his hat and Griff returned the courtesy.

Small-town America wasn't exactly Lexi's speed.

Downtown Buffalo, going across the border into Canada to try to get into the bars with lower drinking age—*that* he understood. But this?

Griff followed the GPS to Main Street. Several storefronts stood empty, including one between what appeared to be the hardware store and the diner. He easily found a parking spot in front of the vacant building. He climbed out of the truck and stood on the sidewalk. Yellowing tape adhered newspaper to the cloudy windows, making it impossible to see inside. Unease twisted his gut at the thought of Lexi hanging out here. He tried the front door. Locked.

Come on, Lexi. Where are you?

Cool air had settled in the shadows of the brick building. Not a soul was on the street. Things shut down early around here. He yanked open the door to the diner.

"Sit wherever you'd like," a waitress said, not bothering to stop as she strode toward the counter and set the coffee carafe on the warmer. "I'll be over with a menu in a sec."

Griff slipped into a booth by the window. An elderly couple were the only other diners. His hopes of finding someone who saw Lexi were dashed. Monday wasn't exactly a big go-out-to-dinner night. And there weren't any teenagers hanging out. Perhaps Nick had lied simply to get rid of him.

The waitress wandered over and slid a plastic menu onto the table. "Some big meth bust in one of those abandoned houses on the edge of town?"

Griff furrowed his brow.

She tipped her chin toward his suit coat. "Only reason we ever get Feds around here."

"Nope, not a meth bust." Griff smiled up at the waitress. Her name tag was pinned sideways on her white blouse: *Cailey's* parents spelled their daughter's name in an unconventional way. He'd guess she was Lexi's age.

Cailey raised an eyebrow, apparently waiting for him to give her the dirt.

Griff fumbled with his phone for a second. "Have you seen this girl?"

Cailey angled her head to get a good look at the photo. "Nope." She lifted her wide blue eyes to meet his. "She in trouble?"

"I hope not. She's my niece. I'm worried about her."

"I haven't seen her." She struck him as bored.

"Okay." He handed her a business card. "Would you call me if you do? You probably see a lot here."

"Sure." She turned the card over in her hand, then slipped it into the back pocket of her jeans. Cailey's fingers brushed across the menu. "You gonna order?" The slight downturn at the corners of her mouth suggested she feared missing out on a tip.

The ceiling lights reflected off the shiny menu. A picturesque club sandwich made his stomach growl. He had been so worried about Lexi, he hadn't realized how hungry he was. He didn't have any other leads, so it wasn't like he was wasting time. "I'll take the club sandwich and a water."

The waitress scribbled on her pad. "Okeydokey." She spun around and her blonde ponytail swished behind her. The elderly couple talked quietly while sharing a piece of pie. He'd wait until they were done before he disturbed them.

Shortly after Cailey delivered his dinner, a young woman walked into the diner. She strode directly to the counter. Her confidence suggested she had been here many times, a local most likely, but definitely not Amish. Not with her long, silky dark hair and figure-hugging jeans.

Don't be that guy.

He picked up a napkin and wiped his fingers. Just in case this woman was grabbing an order to go, he wanted to catch her before she left. Griff slid out of the booth and strolled over to the counter and plopped down on the stool, leaving one empty between them. "Hello."

"Hi." The woman gave him a half-smile that didn't reach her brown eyes. She braced her forearms on the narrow counter and called into the kitchen. "Is my order ready?"

The waitress strode toward the swinging door. "Micky went out for a smoke break, but I'm pretty sure he already packed your order."

"Thanks." The woman slid off the stool and made a show of studying the photos on the wall. She obviously wasn't interested in small talk.

"Excuse me." Griff stood and approached her. "I'm looking for my niece. Maybe you've seen her." He held out his smartphone. Lexi's beautiful smile beamed up at him.

The woman turned toward him. For the first time, the hard set of her mouth softened as they locked gazes. "Yeah, sure." She lowered her eyes to the photo but seemed a million miles away. "I'm sorry. She doesn't look familiar." Concern creased the skin between her perfectly arched brows. "Is she in danger?"

"I don't know. Her mother tracked her cell phone to this area."

"Did you find it?" Something he couldn't quite pinpoint flashed in the woman's eyes.

"Yes, she left it in the back of a cab. Well, more like one of those private, independent outfits. The guy's son told me they cater to the Amish."

The woman's jaw slackened. "It didn't happen to be the Gilmores out on Potter Road?" Pink crawled up her cheeks and a wariness that further unnerved him settled in her eyes.

"Yes, it was." He searched her face, hoping this was finally the connection to his niece he had been searching for. "Are you familiar with the service? Is there something sketchy going on here?"

"I do know the family. Chester and his son, Nicky." She opened her mouth as if to say more, then snapped it shut. "But I haven't seen your niece." The woman raised her voice and directed it toward the back. "Hey Cailey, you have my order there?"

The waitress pushed through the doors with a bright smile and a brown bag with a big grease stain. "Here you go."

The customer slipped two fingers into the tight front pocket of her jeans and pulled out a twenty. She set the folded bill on the counter.

Cailey picked it up and spun around to the register. "Let me get your change."

"We're all good here." She grabbed the takeout bag and Griff suspected he had struck out yet again. However, she gestured toward the exit with a tip of her head. "We should talk in private."

"Sure." Griff followed her out onto Main Street, praying this would somehow lead him to Lexi. The mention of the Gilmores had lit a fire in her eyes.

CHAPTER 6

*S*arah led the stranger into the hardware store two doors down from the diner. Gramps pushed away heavily from his perch on the stool behind the counter, ready to offer directions to an item or tips on a home improvement project. The deep lines at the corners of his eyes struck her heart with sadness. He seemed so tired. Weary, almost. How much longer would he be able to work these long shifts? She hadn't exactly taken him for granted, but selfishly she had figured he'd be here forever. Her rock.

The haze of melancholy dissipated when her grandpa's welcoming smile transformed his face. He nodded at his granddaughter and his gaze quickly drifted to the man behind her. He was ready to spring into "Welcome, can I help you find anything?" mode.

"He's with me, Gramps." Sarah plunked the brown takeout bag on the counter. Then she turned toward the man and smiled, feeling a little foolish for being rude. She held out her hand. "Sarah James."

His encircled hers with a firm grip. "Trevor Griffin."

She tipped her head toward Gramps. "This is my grandfather, Russ Bennett. He owns the store."

The two men shook hands. "Nice to meet you," Trevor said.

Her grandpa narrowed his gaze and angled his head. "Is something wrong? You're with law enforcement, right?"

Sarah gave Trevor a quizzical look. "I thought you were looking for your niece?"

"I am. I'm also with the FBI, but I'm not here in an official capacity." He plucked at his suit coat. "I came directly from the office after my sister called. She hasn't seen her daughter since Saturday morning."

A growing dread hollowed out Sarah's stomach. "It's Monday night." Then she gave herself a mental shake for being judgmental. "How old is she?"

"Lexi's eighteen."

"Ah… Has she done this before?" Sarah studied Trevor's face. His warm, brown eyes held a deep concern. He obviously loved his niece very much.

"Unfortunately, yes. But never for this long." He crossed his arms over his broad chest and the movement of his suit coat revealed a gun. Perhaps help, in the form of an FBI agent, had just walked into her life. But would he be interested in helping her find Hannah when he was looking for his niece? Something in her gut told her they might be able to help one another. They already had the Gilmores in common. And that wasn't necessarily a good thing.

Gramps planted his palm on the counter, his arm a little shaky. "I'm sorry to hear your niece is missing." Hand still in place, he pivoted to make eye contact with Sarah. "Did you know this girl?"

"No, Gramps."

Her grandpa had only been peripherally aware of her work to help the Amish until this past summer. She had preferred it that way. She never wanted to force Gramps to lie in order to protect her. But her mission had come under the glaring spotlight of the local sheriff's department when her involvement in helping a young Amish woman disappear became entangled in their efforts to find a deranged stalker. Fortunately, the creep was arrested, Hannah was safe—or so everyone thought—and Sarah was held blameless.

But now Hannah's whereabouts were in question again.

Maybe it was time to stop interfering.

Sarah lifted the takeout bag. "I'll walk you upstairs."

Gramps smiled. "I can find my way upstairs." He pointed a shaky finger at her. "Help him find his niece."

"I'll do what I can." She felt Trevor's curious gaze on her.

The agent took a step toward her grandpa. "Before you go, maybe you can take a look…" He reached into his coat pocket and pulled out his smartphone. He swiped his finger across the screen and held it up. "Does she look familiar? I tracked her cell to Chester Gilmore's place on Potter Road. I understand he provides rides to the Amish."

"Nicky claims his dad picked her up," Sarah added.

"Sorry, I don't recognize her." Gramps blinked slowly and swayed.

She scooted behind the counter and slid her hand around the crook of his arm. He had mentioned being light-headed last week but refused to go to the doctor's. "Are you okay?"

Her grandpa waved her away. "Fine, fine. Just hungry. That's all." He gave her a mischievous smile. He was fiercely independent, which proved problematic at times. She'd have to be more vigilant about making sure he ate at regular intervals.

Sarah turned to Trevor. "Give me a minute. I'll be right back."

"You don't have to help me. I've been living here and climbing these stairs my entire life." He took the takeout bag from Sarah, perhaps a little too forcefully. "I'll say a prayer that you find your niece safe and sound. If you print out some photos, I'd be happy to post them in my shop window."

"Thank you." Trevor slipped his phone into his pocket.

"Now, if you'll excuse me. I'm starving." Gramps's tone held a lightness that Sarah wasn't buying. He turned and shuffled toward the back stairs.

"I'm not going upstairs because of you," Sarah said. "I need to get some water. Would you like some water, agent?"

"Um, sure." He tipped his head almost imperceptibly, as if to say, *Go, do what you have to do, I'll be here.*

Sarah climbed the steps behind her grandpa. His grip on the railing was tight as he pulled himself up. He had done this for as long as she could remember, but tonight he seemed older to her. "You feel okay, Gramps?" she asked again, hoping he'd be honest with her without an audience.

"Just hungry. That's all. I told you." He rarely snapped at her, which put her further on edge, but she knew she wasn't going to get anything more from him.

He maneuvered across the small apartment, touching the back of the kitchen chair, the sofa, until he got to his comfy recliner stationed in front of the TV. He placed the food on the TV tray set up next to the chair. He reached for the remote. He recorded *Nightly News with Lester Holt* so he could watch it at the end of the day.

"Go, don't leave the gentleman waiting downstairs." He lifted his eyes to meet hers. "I hope if you had a hand in this, you'd tell that man. He's worried about his niece."

"I don't know anything about his niece. But I *am* concerned about a major coincidence."

"Coincidence?"

"I ran into Annie Yutzy at the grocery store, and she said Hannah Shetler was headed home. Apparently, Chester Gilmore gave her a ride, but no one in Hunters Ridge has seen her. Maybe she wasn't really going home. What if she was lying?" Sarah shrugged, weighing the nonthreatening options. "Considering the many changes in her life, it wouldn't be out of the question."

"Maybe it's time you stopped meddling in the affairs of the Amish."

Sarah rubbed the back of her neck, then pointed the remote at the TV and turned on the evening news.

"They are not you," Gramps said. "They choose to live separate."

Her heart sank—this was the first time her grandpa had expressed a strong negative opinion about her work. Embarrassment—or maybe it was shame—heated her face. She had always believed her work to be noble. She knew what it was like to feel trapped. Her overbearing father made sure of it. She thanked God every day that her grandpa took her in when her own mother wouldn't stand up to him. Then, when an Amish friend committed suicide...

She let the thought trail off. No one could prove that her friend knew she was walking out onto thin ice—literally—but Sarah had a hard time reconciling the risky act with her friend's cautious temperament. The same temperament that had convinced her she had no other choice but to stay in Hunters Ridge and live a life she hated.

Sarah *had* to help young women who wanted to leave the Amish way. They might live separate, but it wasn't always of their choosing. She cleared her throat. This conversation would take more time than she had right now. "We'll talk later, Gramps. Love you." She reached for the door.

Without turning his face away from Lester Holt, Gramps asked, "What about your water?"

Sarah shook her head tightly, as if just now remembering the water she had never intended on getting. She grabbed two bottles from the fridge and headed downstairs, still feeling uneasy about Gramps's health.

"Everything okay?" The agent hadn't moved more than a foot from where he had been standing when she went upstairs.

She studied him for a moment. His sandy-brown hair was cut short. Perhaps he had served time in the military, or maybe it was just the FBI vibe she was feeling. She suspected he had been clean-shaven this morning, but the dark shadow of a long day emphasized his square jaw. Her assessment of him dragged on a beat too long and she lowered her gaze, her face burning. "Yeah, he's just..." Goodness, he didn't really care how her grandfather was doing. This man had to find his niece. "Anyway, you said she left her phone in the Gilmores' van."

"You know the Gilmores?"

"Yes." She tucked a strand of hair behind her ear. Nick Gilmore had been a client of hers when he was twelve years old, but she couldn't share that information. "Coincidentally, I'm also looking for a missing girl. Woman, really. She decided to leave the Amish."

He watched her expectantly.

"Last I heard, she had taken a ride from Chester Gilmore while on her way back home."

Trevor fisted his hand and a muscle ticked in his jaw. "Is the sheriff's department involved?"

Sarah slowly shook her head. "No, not really. All evidence points to Hannah leaving on her own." She gave him the short version of a long, convoluted story. "Her neighbor is a sheriff's deputy. She said she'd make a few calls. Hannah may have changed her mind about coming home. Perhaps she was unwilling to face the consequences of leaving the Amish community in the first place. I only learned this today and I haven't had a chance to talk to Chester."

"Chester's out of town," the agent said.

"You talked to Nick, then?" Sarah's heart raced in her chest. She remembered him as the little boy with dark hair hanging in his face. He never lifted his head to meet her gaze. He had given her the creeps, but as a professional, she tried to reach the young boy who had recently lost his mother and had taken on some disturbing habits. Chester had stopped bringing his son to her when she advised him to seek help from someone with more credentials. As far as she knew, Nick never saw anyone else.

"I did talk to Nick. He claimed Lexi's phone had been left in the van. He also said he didn't know when his father would be home and he had no way to reach him. Don't you find that odd?"

Yes. "Chester and Nick don't have the best of relationships." At least, they hadn't. She was careful with what she revealed. "It wouldn't surprise me. He'd be happy to have the place to himself."

"Did you reach out to her family?" The agent rubbed a hand across his jaw.

"Yes, but that dynamic is even more difficult than Nick and Chester's relationship."

"How so?"

"How much do you know about the Amish?"

He shook his head. "Not much. Just what I've seen on TV."

"Well, they are strict and don't take kindly to those who run away."

The door swung open and the deep hum of a damaged car muffler filled the space. Sarah smiled tightly at the customer, trying to hide her annoyance at being interrupted.

"Excuse me a minute." She approached the man who looked a little lost. "Can I help you find something?"

"Um, yeah." He frowned. "I need to," his eyes drifted to the paint swatches that covered a section of the wall inside the doorway, "pick out a paint color for the exterior of my house."

Sarah held out her palm. "The exterior paints are marked. We can also mix any color you want if you bring in a swatch."

The deep line on his forehead convinced her he didn't spend his weekends plopped down in front of the DIY channels.

"If you bring in a sample of the color you want, my grandpa can tint the paint to match."

The young man took off his baseball cap, scratched his head, then adjusted the cap back in place with both hands. Sarah didn't recognize him, which was unusual for a small town. Then again, her grandpa usually worked the front of the store while she took care of the books or saw clients in the small office at the back of the store.

"You have a look and I'll be back in a minute."

Sarah returned to the agent and directed him toward the back of the store, out of earshot of the customer. "Any chance your niece ditched her phone because she knew her mom was tracking it?" The coincidence of Hannah and his niece going missing after both had called the Gilmore ride service didn't sit well with her. But maybe it was just that—a coincidence. They had to rule out all the obvious scenarios first.

"Lexi was glued to that phone. She'd flip once she realized she had left it in the van, and she'd move heaven and earth to get back to it. The fact that she didn't has me concerned."

"What was your take on Nick Gilmore?"

Trevor twisted his mouth, seeming to weigh his response. "He's a little awkward. I got the sense he's isolated out there."

Valid assessment.

"Do you know him?" His watchful gaze warmed her skin.

"It's a small town," she whispered so as not to be overheard by the customer.

"Tell me about him." He matched her hushed tone and the deep rumble of his voice seemed almost intimate.

Sarah drew in a deep breath and let it out, hoping to shake the effect he was having on her. She didn't put much emphasis on dating and only did so casually. Apparently, she needed to get out more. "There's not much to tell. I've seen him in the diner with his dad. He's quiet. He prefers video games to interacting with people." Sarah shrugged. "That's about it." Or at least, that's all she could share without violating professional ethics. She cleared her throat and asked, "Have *you* called the sheriff's department?" She glanced toward the front of the store. The customer had a fistful of paint swatches and a concerned look on his face. She sensed he'd be back in here with his wife before he made a selection.

"Not yet. I'm hoping I can sort this out myself, but I do have resources at my disposal."

"Why isn't her disappearance FBI business?" Sarah crossed her arms.

"She's taken off with friends before. Always comes back. But this feels different. And the phone thing has us rattled."

"You could call the sheriff. They'd look into it." Sarah studied his unreadable face. "Better safe than sorry, right?"

"It's complicated." Sarah sensed she wasn't the only one holding back. "I'm going to look for her first. If she doesn't show up soon, then we'll weigh our options."

Sarah glanced at the clock over her shoulder. "I have to keep the store open until nine, but we need to go back to the Gilmores' house. Talk to Nick again." Another hour. It would be dark by then. A whisper of dread made the fine hairs on the back of her neck stand on edge. She had been taught that it was rude to show up unannounced, but if anyone could get Nicky to talk, it would be her.

"I don't think Nick's a chatty kid. We won't get much more out of him."

Sarah squared her shoulders. "We can help each other, agent."

"Call me Griff." He must have noticed the slight twitch of her eyebrow, so he added, "Short for Griffin."

Sarah laughed. "Yeah, of course." She held up her index finger in a *hold on a minute* gesture. She strode toward the front of the store and looked around. The customer had left. Strange that she hadn't noticed. She slipped in behind the counter. "We'll go to the Gilmores' at nine."

"Sounds good," Griff said distractedly, his focus shifting to the screen of his phone.

Good, maybe I won't have to make small talk until closing time.

Sarah sat down on Gramps's stool. Her attention drifted toward the window overlooking Main Street. A growing dread knotted her stomach. Had evil once again found its way to Hunters Ridge?

CHAPTER 7

With her back against a hay bale, Hannah hugged her legs to her chest and rested her forehead on her knees. She'd never get used to this dark, damp barn loft, her prison since her foolish attempt to escape. At least before, she had free rein of the house and a soft bed to sleep in. That was before she realized she only had the illusion of freedom. He had been watching her, ready to snatch her if she dared to leave.

A soft moaning sound made her lift her head. The new girl had been sleeping since she arrived—maybe two nights ago—and had been rustling for the past hour or so. Everything was hazy. Relief competed with the ball of anxiety knotting her stomach. The way he had carried her up the ladder to the loft, like a fireman, her limp body slung over his shoulder—she'd feared the girl was dead. Maybe he had lured her here the same way he had her, with the promise of a housekeeping job. Or maybe he had drugged her immediately, understanding that an *Englisch* girl wouldn't be so easily duped. The start of a prayer formed on her lips, but she stopped herself. Anger bubbled up instead. She had been praying nonstop.

She had prayed for the opportunity to escape.

She had prayed when her plans had been foiled.

She had prayed, prayed, prayed…and nothing. If her faith hadn't been destroyed during her struggle with the Amish way, it certainly hadn't been strengthened by her current predicament.

White moonlight filtered in through the spaces between the wood planks shrunken from age and sun. If she could find gratitude, it would be for the rainless night. The constant drip, drip, drip had finally stopped.

Her new roommate blinked a few times, then her eyes widened, and she pushed up on her elbow. Another groan escaped her lips. "Where… What…?"

Hannah couldn't be sure, but she thought the girl swore under her breath. If an *Englischer* was going to swear, Hannah figured now was as good a time as any. "You're in a barn in Hunters Ridge."

The girl narrowed her gaze, an angry expression flashing in her eyes. "Why?" Hannah suspected the raspiness in the girl's voice was from days of not talking. "Why? Who did this?"

She pushed to a seated position and swayed, obviously still loopy from whatever the man had given her. She braced her arms on either side of her and straightened her legs. The line of moonlight slashing her face revealed the exact moment she discovered what Hannah had already known. She had a shackle around her ankle and the chain was attached to a reinforced steel ring connected to a wood plank.

"What the heck?" The girl shot a glance toward Hannah, then seemed to take in her Amish attire for the first time, and lowered her eyes. "Sorry, I didn't mean to offend you."

"No apology required." Hannah shouldn't have been so happy for company. "My name's Hannah."

"Lexi." She dropped down to the loft floor and rested her back against the hay bale facing Hannah. Her hand snagged on knots as she dragged it through her long hair. "How long have I been here?"

Hannah rubbed her forehead. She had lost all sense of time since she had been moved here from the main house after her failed escape. Had it been days? Weeks? A fogginess clouded her brain. Perhaps she had lain sleeping for days like Lexi. This realization made her thinking fuzzier. Had she been here even longer than she thought? "I'm not sure. Two nights?"

"Two nights?" Alarm made her voice squeak. She glanced around as if answers might reveal themselves in the shadows of the musty-smelling barn.

"You've been sleeping," Hannah said.

Lexi licked her lips. "More like drugged."

Hannah couldn't help but wonder how she had figured that out so quickly. It'd taken her a while to realize he must have done something to her to make her feel so disoriented.

Hannah watched the girl's heavily shadowed face. "Do you know when you were taken?" *Taken.* It seemed like such an innocent word.

"I called for a ride on Saturday." She exhaled on a shaky breath, as if realizing that had been her mistake.

"Saturday night?"

"Yeah, I had been hanging out with some friends in Jamestown. I couldn't get an Uber, so I asked around. A couple Amish girls were sitting in the fast-food restaurant. They gave me a number for a ride. They told me it was safe. They used the service all the time." There was a faraway quality to her voice. "I figured I'd find a cheap motel."

57

"Don't you have a home?" Hannah blurted out the question before she had a chance to second-guess herself.

"Yeah, but I didn't want to go there. Too much drama." The short sentence held the weight of heavy regret.

"What else do you remember?"

Lexi scratched her head. "Nothing. I called for a ride. The van showed up…" The chain on Lexi's leg rattled as she drew her knees to her chest. Suddenly she patted the back of her jeans. "Did you see my phone?"

Hannah shook her head.

"Yeah, that would have been a nice stroke of luck." Lexi slumped against the hay bale.

Hannah didn't believe in luck, and it wasn't because she was Amish. Her life, of late, had shown her how fickle fate could be.

"I should have stayed with my friends." Lexi ran the back of her hand under her nose. "I'm so stupid."

"Don't say that."

Lexi looked up and paused, then bowed her head. "Do you remember how you got here? Maybe we can find a way out." Her hopeful tone was heartbreaking.

Hannah lifted her foot and yanked, reminding her new mate that they weren't going anywhere. "I called for a ride, too." That was the short version. "I had left the Amish earlier this summer, but I missed my family. After I climbed into the van, he told me his family needed a housekeeper. He suggested I come by and see his home." Her laugh sounded brittle in her ears. "I thought if I had a job, I wouldn't feel so trapped." She shrugged. "It's not like I'm going to get married anytime soon. Money would give me options to leave again when I was really ready, but I'd be close enough to see my brothers whenever I wanted." If her father didn't forbid it.

Lexi rested her crossed arms on her bent knees.

"I soon learned he already had live-in help."

"There's someone else here?" Lexi straightened her legs and the metal chain rattled.

A new wave of shame heated Hannah's cheeks. "*Yah.* I only hope I haven't put her in jeopardy when I tried to leave."

"Wait, wait…you tried to escape?" Lexi tugged on the solid chain. "How?"

"He allowed me to live in the main house. Once I realized he wasn't all that he claimed to be, I slipped out the front door at night. But he was waiting for me." She closed her eyes and drew in a calming breath. "Then he moved me here and chained me up. Then you showed up."

"Yeah, well, not because I wanted to. Trust me." Lexi's tone dripped with sarcasm, giving Hannah hope that her new roommate would have the spark she needed to survive. She ran a hand over her face and her voice grew shaky. "What does he want with us?"

A shudder raced up Hannah's spine. "I don't know."

"The guy's a sicko. He had these chains installed to keep women here. This isn't good. He's been planning this for a while. We *have* to get out of here." Lexi seemed to be thinking out loud, mirroring many of the same thoughts Hannah had struggled with alone. And as much as she liked having company, she wouldn't have wished this nightmare on anyone.

Hannah touched the shackle on her ankle. Her skin was tender from tugging at it over the past few days.

Lexi pushed off the floor and followed the chain to where it was attached to the wall. "I'm not gonna let this sicko do whatever he has planned for us." She yanked on the chain and groaned. She slowly turned around. "Did he…" She cleared her throat. "Did he do *anything* to you?"

Heat tinged Hannah's cheeks, and she gingerly touched the strings on her bonnet. *I don't think so. I pray he didn't. I can't remember.* But she had been thinking clearer now that she had stopped eating the tainted food. "No," she said with a conviction she didn't feel. She had been in sweatpants and a T-shirt when she'd tried to make her escape, but now she had on her plain clothes. *Did he...?* She shook the thought away. *No.* She'd know if he did something. She'd feel different if he had, right?

Lexi's expression softened in the lines of moonlight. "Maybe the other girl got away. Maybe she's getting help."

Hannah stifled a shudder, choosing not to tell Lexi that the other girl had been far too timid to risk getting help. Maybe he had warned her that she'd end up here. She had tried to convince Hannah not to leave... She should have listened.

She should have listened a long time ago. She had been disobedient. Defied the *Ordnung*. She should have never run away from home in the first place.

Now she'd likely pay with her life.

Hannah closed her eyes and rested her cheek on her knees. A bucket sat in the corner and she felt her stomach lurch. Shame and fear twined up her backbone.

A deep rumbling vibrated through the loft floor. Hannah leaned forward and in an urgent voice, she whispered. "Lexi, listen to me." Her ears perked at the sound of footsteps swooshing through long grass. "You have to listen. He's coming."

Lexi yelped quietly. She darted toward Hannah, but the shackles sent her reeling backward.

Hannah crawled toward her. "Don't let him know you're afraid," she whispered, then lay on the floor, her back resting against a hay bale. She wanted—no, needed—for him to think she was out of it. Weak. Easy prey. She had given this a lot of thought. It was her last hope.

Hannah studied Lexi's profile through slitted eyes.

The scraping of wood against the earth indicated he was

dragging the ladder to access the loft. A thud sounded as the ladder made contact with the edge. Each rung creaked under his weight as he climbed.

"What do you want from me, sicko?" Lexi shouted at him.

He pulled himself up onto the loft and set down a brown bag. Food. He covered the small space in three awkward steps and pressed his hand against Lexi's mouth. Muffled mewls escaped from under his hand. Hannah's heart raced. Someone must be close by. Hope blossomed in her chest. She had never seen him worried about noise.

"Shut up." He gave her a hard shake. "Do you hear me? Shut up!"

Hannah felt like a traitor, lying here motionless. But she knew she'd be of no help to the *Englischer*. Her shackles limited her range of motion.

Seemingly satisfied that the girl would be quiet, he lowered his hand. "Someone came looking for you today." There was a gleeful quality to his voice.

"My mom?" Lexi sounded far younger than Hannah imagined she was.

"Not Mommy." He was obviously enjoying toying with her.

"Who?"

"Your uncle came sniffing around today."

"My phone app—" Lexi said before she had a chance to stop herself.

"Yup. Big Brother at its finest. He tracked your phone to my house. But no worries. I told him you left it in the van when my father picked you up." He shrugged. Such a casual gesture for an unhinged man. "Happens all the time. People are careless."

Lexi hiked her chin in defiance. "He'll find me. He's an FBI agent. He's good at that sort of—"

The man spun around and jabbed his finger at her. "He's not smarter than me."

A hollowness swelled inside Hannah. Was anyone looking for her? Not likely. Her father would be ashamed of her. He wouldn't waste his energy searching for her. A single tear leaked from the corner of her eye. She resisted the urge to wipe it away. She didn't want the man to know she was awake. Listening.

He shuffled backward toward the ladder. "Keep your mouths shut or I'll slap duct tape over your lips." He pointed at Lexi. "Makes no difference to me." He stopped and cocked his head. Something had drawn his attention toward Hannah.

She kept still, watching him through her eyelashes.

He crouched down in front of her. Her heart nearly exploded in her chest. "It won't be easy to breathe with your mouth taped shut."

It took everything Hannah had not to move away from him, not that she could go far. She'd likely flail like a hooked fish on the deck of a boat.

He jabbed his index finger into her thigh. "I know you're awake."

He hovered over her for a long moment, before pivoting and leaving the same way he had come. The same way he always came.

Bits of damp hay bit into her hand as she pushed off the loft floor into a seated position. Despite her rioting nerves, she realized she was hungry. But since the only way to get food was from him, she'd rather starve.

Lexi tore into the bag.

"We can't eat that!" Hannah whispered harshly in case the man was lurking nearby.

The girl froze. "Why not?"

"He puts something in it."

"Like drugs?" Lexi sat back on her heels. "Great. I'm starving."

"I kept falling asleep after I ate and then felt groggy. So if we have any hope of getting out of here, we have to stay alert."

Lexi picked up the bag of food and threw it against the barn wall. It landed with a thud behind a hay bale. The image of rats scurrying around their shared space was the least of Hannah's concerns.

CHAPTER 8

*T*he next morning, Sarah made sure Gramps had everything he needed, then she stepped outside the hardware store and found Griff parked by the curb. She climbed in and snapped the buckle. "Morning." She ran her hands up and down her thighs, unable to still the hum of nerves vibrating through her. They had tried to contact Nick Gilmore last night, but he never answered the door.

"How'd you sleep?"

"Fine." She opted for the polite answer. In reality, she'd spent a restless night wondering how Griff's niece and Hannah were both tied to the Gilmores. She struggled with not telling Griff that Nicky had been one of her clients. She was bound by confidentiality and hadn't convinced herself that he was a danger to anyone. Not yet. "How about you?" she asked. "We don't exactly have five-star accommodations in town."

"Hunters Ridge Motel is clean and had a bed. I don't need much more." He tapped the two lids on plain white cups in the cupholders. "Even have coffee."

Sarah laughed. "Gourmet, I'm sure."

"It gets the job done. Got one for you." He peeled back the cover on the console revealing cream and sugar packets.

"Thanks."

"How's your grandfather?" he asked as he checked the mirrors and pulled out onto Main Street.

"Good." She left the coffee in the holder and took off the lid. She dumped in two sugars. "I don't know how he does it. He's been working at that hardware store since he was old enough to hold a job." She added a creamer. Then another. "I'd be bored out of my mind."

"I imagine it was busier in past years."

Sarah tipped her head. "I suppose so." She stopped herself, feeling disrespectful to Gramps, a man she loved dearly and who'd provided for her when she most needed it.

"Why do you stay in Hunters Ridge?" Griff asked the obvious question.

"My grandfather. He'd be alone without me." There was so much more to it, but she didn't make it a habit to unload on virtual strangers. However, it seemed their situation had allowed them to form a quick bond. She poured her third sugar packet into the coffee and stirred it with the short stick. Griff had thought of everything. She took a sip. *Perfect.* "And people in small towns need social workers, too."

"Do you have a lot of clients?"

"Enough." Her mind drifted to a nervous Hannah who had met her in the back office. She had dropped off pies to sell at the diner, then came into the hardware store and bought something small like a potholder or duct tape in case someone asked why she had stopped there. Hannah had been conflicted about fleeing the Amish and had cut her therapy sessions short, leaving Sarah to believe she had decided to stay in Hunters Ridge. Instead, she had jumped the fence in the middle of the night.

Sarah stared out the passenger window. Another image

floated to mind. One of a twelve-year-old Nicky Chester sitting in her office. His father sat next to him growing angrier and angrier as the preteen slumped and his unkempt hair fell into his eyes.

"The kid better answer the door this morning," Griff said, snapping her out of her reverie.

"It's early. He'll be home." She shifted in her seat so her knees faced him. She took a sip of her coffee.

"You seem pretty confident about that."

"You seem confident he had something to do with your niece's disappearance."

Griff slanted her a side-eye. "How well do you know this kid?"

She lifted an eyebrow, hoping that was enough of a tell without actually spelling it out.

"I need to be concerned?" Griff asked.

Sarah placed her coffee in the holder and lifted her eyes to meet his. "Let's just say Nicky has issues. I shouldn't say more."

"Okay." Griff cleared his throat and adjusted his grip on the steering wheel. "*Nicky* had Lexi's phone. It's the only lead I have."

Sarah drummed her fingers on her thigh, debating with herself. *Screw it.* Griff was law enforcement. It wasn't like she was gossiping about her clients in the middle of the diner. "Nicholas Gilmore killed the family dog when he was a kid."

Griff groaned and he cut his gaze toward Sarah. A fraction too long. She jammed a finger toward the windshield. "Watch!"

He tugged the steering wheel to the left to avoid hitting the Amish wagon making its way along the side of the road. "Thanks." Staring straight ahead, he asked, "Like, he accidentally backed over his beloved pet when he first got his license?" The wariness in his tone suggested he already knew the answer.

"No. Intentionally and violently." The anguish on Mr. Gilmore's face was etched in her memory. The elder Gilmore had been recently widowed and didn't have a handle on his son.

"Oh, man." Griff scrubbed a hand across his clean-shaven face. She could smell his aloe aftershave. "There was a dog at the house yesterday."

"Of course there was. After his father's initial shock wore off, he dismissed his son's violent behavior as grief. After a few visits, they stopped coming. I wanted to believe he lost his propensity for violence."

"How likely is that?" Griff slowed and glanced over at her.

"Turn here." Sarah straightened in her seat and pointed to the right. "It's a shortcut to Potter Road."

"Okay."

"And regarding Nicky's violent tendencies, it's highly unlikely he's changed without major intervention." She ran a hand over her lips. "I hope he's not abusing his current dog."

"Yeah." Griff sighed heavily. "And I pray he hasn't moved on to bigger targets."

A cold chill skittered down her spine. She watched the Gilmores' home come into view. It had fallen into disrepair. She wondered what Mrs. Gilmore would think of her family home. Sarah absentmindedly ran her fingers back and forth on the armrest. "That's why I had to tell you about his history."

"I appreciate it. I pray that he's kept his nose clean."

Me, too.

They turned into the driveway. "Hey, that van wasn't there yesterday. Maybe Nicky's father is back in town." Hope edged Griff's voice.

They both climbed out of the truck and approached the

front porch. No one answered their repeated knocking despite the incessant barking on the other side of the door. At least the dog was okay.

"Maybe his father got in late and they're both sleeping." Griff stepped off the porch and moved toward the van.

"You'd think they'd want to know what has their dog riled up." Sarah shaded her eyes and looked up at the second-story windows. No movement. "This doesn't feel right." She slapped at a mosquito on her arm.

"I agree." Griff cupped his hand to the window of the van. Nothing unusual.

The side door facing the driveway creaked open. Nicky's pinched face appeared in the crack.

"Hi, Nicky," Sarah said warmly.

"What's going on?" He didn't open the door any wider.

"Can we talk to your dad?" Sarah gestured to the van with her thumb. "I see he's back."

One visible brow drew down. "I hadn't realized so many people were tracking my dad's movements."

"Can we talk to him? I'd really like to get more information about where he dropped off my niece." Gravel crunched under Griff's shoes as he crossed the driveway to the side door.

"Let me see if he's awake." Nicky slammed the door shut. The dog's barking sounded deeper in the house. A few minutes later he returned and opened the door wider. The young man was dressed in gray joggers and a soiled white T-shirt. "He's sleeping. He said to give him a call in a few hours."

"It's important," Griff insisted. "Does he know that?"

Nicky leaned against the doorframe and made a drinking gesture. "I think you'll get better information out of him later."

Griff stepped back, frustrated. "You still have my card?" Nicky nodded. "Have him call me as soon as he sobers up."

Nicky gave Griff a mock salute, then cut her a sideways glare.

Sarah had a small practice, but Nicky would rank up there as one of her top five clients—maybe top two—who made her feel uncomfortable. He had a way of looking through her. A way of smiling at her and threatening her at the same time. A way of appearing to agree with authority while completely disregarding it. They weren't going to get any further with him today. They'd have to wait until his father sobered up and gave Griff a call.

After leaving the Gilmores' house, Griff and Sarah spent the day exploring every possible place a teenager who was trying to stay under the radar might hang out—from the rutted parking lot next to the abandoned restaurant in the middle of nowhere to the steep stairs at the back of the church where kids could perform skateboard tricks and then post their wipeouts online in the hopes of going viral. All the places Sarah could think of were deserted. Apparently, the novelty of a new school year hadn't worn off on the kids likely to skip. *Give it time.*

Canvassing the high school with a photo of his niece at dismissal had been a bust, too. With each dead-end, his dread grew.

Where are you, Lexi?

As the dinner hour approached, Griff realized they hadn't had anything since their coffee this morning. "Care to grab dinner at the diner?"

"Sure. Let me stop in to say hello to Gramps first."

Griff parked in front of the hardware store. When they

went inside, Sarah's grandpa was holding court with two other gentlemen. Sarah gave each of the elderly men a warm, one-armed hug and greeted them by name.

The gentleman in the red golf shirt smiled and said, "We tried to pry Russ out of here to check out that new restaurant in Jamestown, but you know him…"

"I do." Sarah glanced around. "I can take over if you guys want to go out."

Gramps held up his hand. "No, no, don't you go siding with them. I'm fine here."

"You never go out. Go!" Sarah had seemed to forget about their plans for the diner, but he understood her change of heart.

The three gentlemen moved their gaze to Griff. The man closest to Sarah nudged her with his elbow. "We wouldn't want to ruin your date."

Griff opened his mouth, but then snapped it shut, enjoying watching Sarah squirm. The flawless skin on her cheeks held a rosy glow. She bowed her head and a long, silky strand of brown hair slipped out from behind her delicate ear, which had also pinkened. Fortunately, Sarah was too distracted to notice his smile.

"He's not my…" Sarah shook her head and scooted behind the counter. "Go. Have dinner with your friends. I've got this." She made a shoeing gesture with her hands and amusement lit her eyes. She was obviously used to teasing from her grandfather's friends.

Sarah's entire face beamed as her grandfather's friends ushered him out the door. She truly loved her grandpa. What Griff wouldn't do to have a woman like her look at him like that. Her gaze shifted to him and he immediately schooled his expression. Thank goodness she couldn't read his thoughts.

"I'm sorry," she said. "We were going to have dinner,

weren't we? It's just that Gramps rarely takes time for himself."

"No problem. I'll get takeout. Bring it back."

"You don't have to," Sarah said as she adjusted her position on the stool.

"I'd like to."

Half of Sarah's mouth curved into a smile. "I'd love a BLT on wheat toast. Light mayo."

"Got it."

Griff walked over to the diner. On the way back, he heard what sounded like the thumping of bass coming from the vacant building. He slowed, but the newspaper on the windows blocked his view. He tugged on the front door of the building. Still locked.

He was annoyed with himself for not finding a way to explore this building earlier when Nick first mentioned that kids hung out here. But hadn't he said druggies? That wasn't Lexi. Not at all. For that reason alone, part of him wanted to keep on walking.

He had to be sure.

A prickling started in his scalp, like someone was watching him. He craned his neck to check the second story windows. The evening sun made it nearly impossible to see if anyone was standing in the window. The thought made him feel exposed, but he figured the feeling was more the result of fatigue and hunger and not any real threat. But he'd have to check out the building all the same.

When he walked through the front door, Sarah raced to meet him. "Thanks! What do I owe you?"

"I got it. I owe you for showing me the town. I couldn't do this without you."

"Somehow I doubt that, but thanks." Sarah pulled up another stool and set up a picnic of sorts on the glass counter. She gave him that smile again. "I appreciate your going with the flow. Gramps spends all his time here." Her ring clacked against the glass as she tapped it. "I hated for him to miss an opportunity to hang out with his buddies."

"No problem." Griff unwrapped his sandwich.

Truth be told, he preferred the intimacy of this setting versus the diner. They could talk without being overheard. He was here to find his niece, but he found he was enjoying Sarah's company. Perhaps too much.

"What's going on with the building next door?"

"Empty since earlier this year. It used to be a cute little gift shop. Shut down after Christmas. No plans for it as far as I know."

Griff frowned. "Sounds like there's music coming from inside."

"Really? The sheriff's department cleared it out over a month ago. They assured us the building was locked up tight." Sarah set her sandwich down. "Kids were partying in there, but never before dark." A muscle twitched in her forehead, creating a deep line.

"Maybe we should check it out?" The thought of his niece in there twisted his gut. *Mattresses. Needles. Rodent droppings.*

"It couldn't hurt. But if it makes you feel any better, the young men they chased out of the building were all Amish, probably just looking for a place to blow off steam during *Rumspringa.* Harmless. The deputy told me there weren't any drugs. Just some beer cans stacked up."

"Rum-what?" Griff jerked his head back.

"*Rumspringa.* A time for Amish teens to push the boundaries before they get baptized. The elders don't encourage it, but they do tend to look the other way for the most part."

"Interesting." Griff folded a corner of the sandwich wrapper. "The Gilmore kid told me kids did drugs in there."

Sarah pressed her lips together and lifted her shoulders slightly.

"I need to get in there."

"Of course. I would have mentioned it earlier, but I thought the building was secure. It's been quiet since the sheriff's department kicked the boys out." She reached into her purse. "I'll call the sheriff's department."

He placed his hand over hers. "No, I'll take a peek." He'd find a way in.

"Eat first." She smiled mischievously. "If you're a good boy, I'll give you a key to the front door."

"A key to the building next door?"

"Yep." She climbed off the stool and opened a dirt-brown filing cabinet tucked under the counter. She slid all the files forward and pulled out a small metal lockbox. She popped it open and rustled through it before pulling out a key with a cross keychain. She dangled it in front of him. "Gramps and the owner of the building next door were good friends."

Griff took the key and dropped it into his pocket. "That'll make things easier." He took a big bite of his sandwich. Food first, then the vacant building.

Sarah finished half her sandwich, then rolled the remaining half in its wrapper. "Earlier today when I suggested you call the sheriff, you said it was complicated." Her eyes twitched. "I can't imagine why you wouldn't want more resources looking for your niece, even if she has done this before. She's never been gone this long, right?"

"Jeannie, Lexi's mother, is embroiled in a nasty divorce. Nate will use anything he can to gain custody of my nieces to spite my sister. Lexi's old enough to make her own choices, but she has two much younger sisters. I promised her I'd bring Lexi home without involving the police."

Hesitancy lingered in Sarah's eyes, as if she had something on her mind.

"What is it?"

"What if she's in real danger? You should call the sheriff's department."

Renewed anxiety clawed at his chest. "I'm going to give it twenty-four more hours."

"I didn't mean to question your decision. I just hate that these girls are missing." She twisted her pretty lips. "Not to call the kettle black, but the sheriff's department isn't out searching for Hannah, either."

"Why is that again?"

"Because…" Sarah rubbed her knuckles across her cheek. "Really long story, but they were looking for her a few weeks ago. They uncovered a letter in her handwriting, saying that she wanted to leave Hunters Ridge. Case closed."

"Until you ran into the woman who claims Hannah called for a ride home? From the Gilmores."

"Exactly. I talked to one of the deputies. *Unofficially.* They'll keep an eye out, but the sheriff is unlikely to make it a full-blown search. It also doesn't help our cause that Annie is worn out from taking care of her sick husband. Even when I questioned her about Hannah's plans, she got confused. Maybe I'm chasing my tail." Sarah blinked rapidly and turned her face away from him.

"Hey." He reached out and gently touched her chin.

She looked up at him with tears in her eyes. "I'm just tired."

He swiped away a tear with his thumb. "I'll help you find Hannah. You're not alone." Their eyes met and lingered. Sarah was the first to pull away.

She stood and swiped at her wet cheeks. "Your focus needs to be on your niece. I don't want to distract you." Griff studied her for a moment and she quickly added, "…with Hannah. I don't even know if she's in danger."

Griff smiled and patted the keys to the abandoned building next door. "We'll be able to help one another."

And selfishly, he didn't want to do this alone.

CHAPTER 9

*S*arah paced the sidewalk in front of the hardware store trying to burn off nervous energy. Inwardly she cringed. She had made a fool of herself in front of Griff. That's what happened when she was running on fumes. She couldn't control her emotions. Planting her hands on her hips, she drew in a deep breath. Her gaze drifted over to the abandoned building.

What's taking him so long?

She would have gone with him, but she had promised Gramps she'd tend to the store. She stopped and sat down on the bench. They sold the same model. She drummed her fingers on the edge of the seat, unable to remain still. *Come on, Griff, where are you?* The sun had dipped below the horizon and the temperature had also dropped.

A siren sounded in the distance and goose bumps raced up her bare arms. The wailing sound grew louder until a patrol car roared down Main Street and came to a screeching halt in front of the building next door. Heart pounding in her throat, Sarah pushed herself up onto shaky legs.

It had been a long time, but she sent up a silent prayer.

Please let Griff be okay. Her mind had gone to all sorts of dark, horrible places. Had he found something? Someone? *Please, please, please let everyone be okay.*

Her feet felt like anchors of cement, rooting her in place. She stared at the newsprint papering the windows. Deputy Caitlin Flagler climbed out of her patrol car and strode toward the building. She spoke into her shoulder radio, perhaps relaying her location to dispatch. Her exact words were lost in the panic swirling in Sarah's brain. The deputy tipped her head in her direction but made for the front door. The deputy seemed on high alert. She glanced around, then yanked open the door. The newspaper on the glass front door blocked Sarah's view of her as she slipped inside the building where Griff had disappeared.

Unable to wait, Sarah rushed into Gramps's store, grabbed the keys and locked up. As she ran toward the vacant building the door whooshed open. Griff and the deputy stepped outside. Griff was turning something over in his hand.

Fear amplified in her gut. Her words got trapped in her throat.

"Okay," Griff said in response to the deputy.

Deputy Flagler patted Griff on his arm, then walked around to the driver's side of the patrol car. She climbed in but didn't pull away. She typed on the laptop.

"What happened?" Sarah finally found her voice.

Griff looked up at her and blinked, as if he were trying to force himself through a hazy fog. He lifted his hand. He was holding a Hello Kitty wallet. "This is Lexi's. I bought it for her when she was ten."

"Are you sure? She couldn't possibly have been using the same wallet for all these years."

Deep sadness lingered in his brown eyes. He opened the wallet and slid out her New York State license. *Alexis Camp.*

"It's hers. I had to call the sheriff's department. She's in trouble."

Sarah placed her hand on his forearm. The skin over solid muscle was warm. "We'll find her faster this way," she said reassuringly.

"I'm going to send them her photo." He sounded lost, and it broke her heart. "Do you want to include a photo of Hannah?"

Sarah bit her bottom lip to stop it from trembling. She refused to lose it again. "I don't have one." She didn't bother to explain how the Amish didn't like to have their pictures taken. That wasn't his concern right now. "Come on, let me get you something to drink."

Griff bowed his head and jammed his hand through his short, cropped hair. She felt like she was witnessing a rare chink in this man's armor. It made her less self-conscious about her own breakdown earlier. "I have to go to my sister's house. This isn't the kind of news I can deliver over the phone."

"Okay. But Griff—" Sarah paused, forcing him to meet her gaze. "We still don't know anything. It's just her wallet. She might be fine." Her heart ached for Lexi. For Griff. It was human nature to care about the well-being of others, even strangers. But something told her it was more than that. She felt a connection to Griff. A bond. An attraction.

No, no—I'm worried about Lexi. Just the young girl. Please let her be okay.

Griff scratched his eyebrow. "She's run away before, but now that I've found her phone and her wallet..." He visibly shuddered.

"I'm going to drive you to Buffalo."

Griff cleared his throat and squared his shoulders. "I've got this."

"Please, let me do this for you."

He stared at her for a long moment, as if running through how this would work. He nodded almost imperceptibly.

Relief flooded her heart. She patted his arm. "Give me five minutes. I'll meet you by my car in the alley." She forced a smile, resisting the urge to hug him. "It'll be okay."

I have no idea if it will be okay, but it seems like the right thing to say.

Telling his sister that he had found Lexi's wallet in an abandoned building was one of the hardest things Griff had ever had to do. Harder than watching his father waste away from a brain tumor when he was eight. His father made him promise that he would be the man of the house. To this day Griff took that promise seriously.

After making sure his sister had a few friends over for support, he and Sarah grilled three of Lexi's closest friends. Their parents had willingly dragged them out of bed. They seemed to understand that on a different day, at another time, it could be their child.

Now that Lexi's friends knew she could be in real trouble, they'd cough up any secrets they had previously held close out of misguided loyalty.

They learned Lexi had gone to Jamestown, a short drive from Hunters Ridge, to meet a boy she had met online. Unfortunately, her friends didn't know his name, his social media handle, or anything about him. One of her so-called BFFs said she thought Lexi was enjoying the mystery of it all. Griff detected a hint of jealousy in the young girl's tone. As if her feelings were hurt because Lexi had chosen a boy over her.

His head hurt at the recklessness of Lexi's actions. He had warned her ad nauseam about stranger danger. So had her mother. And school. Everyone cautioned kids nowadays. The perils of the internet were not a new thing.

Before Griff and Sarah headed back to Hunters Ridge in the middle of the night with a stack of missing flyers printed out at the FBI's field office in Buffalo, Griff dropped Lexi's cell phone off at a fellow agent's house. He was a superstar hacker, and if anyone could, he'd get into her phone. Griff prayed all their answers were on there. He was also going to unofficially run Nicholas and Chester Gilmore's names through the FBI database. See if they got any hits. He also sent his boss a quick text saying that he'd be taking vacation days through the end of this week. He prayed Lexi would be safe at home by then.

Finally, they jumped on the NYS Thruway headed west to Hunters Ridge. The white dotted line was mesmerizing. He blinked rapidly to fight the sleep that threatened to overtake him at three in the morning.

"Did Chester Gilmore ever call you?" Sarah asked, as if only now thinking about it.

"No, but I told Deputy Flagler that Lexi's cell phone was found at the Potter Road address. She said Nicky has been known to cause trouble around town, but his dad and the sheriff are hunting buddies."

"So, Nicky never suffered any real consequences of his actions."

"Sounds like it. The deputy said she'd drive by. See what Nicky's up to. I haven't heard back from her."

Sarah adjusted the AC and turned the vent away from her face. "Nicky's hiding something."

"It's hard when we have no real proof other than my niece's phone." Griff drummed his fingers on the steering wheel. His eyes felt gritty. "Anyone who can kill their family pet is capable of anything."

Out of the corner of his eye, he saw Sarah shudder. "We need to push Nicky harder."

The headlights illuminated the road, leaving the world beyond in complete blackness. Griff's niece was out there. Somewhere. He gripped the steering wheel tighter. "I don't have time to wait. We're going to have to do anything it takes."

"Like not following the rules."

"Like not following the rules," he repeated.

Sarah dropped off Griff at his truck parked on Main Street. He had wanted to make sure she got inside. She was more insistent, telling him she had made it inside plenty of times before he came along. Reluctantly, he drove away, but not before they made plans to meet at the diner at seven a.m.

A dull headache throbbed behind her eyes as she drove around the block to access the alley that ran behind the hardware store. A glass of water, ibuprofen, and two hours of sleep was all she'd get before she had to do this all over again. She really hoped they'd have more success tomorrow.

She climbed out of her car and clicked the key fob. A quick chirp echoed off the brick walls. A panicked voice in her head urged her to run, run, run.

Stop it.

She fished around in her purse for the keys to the alley door to her second-story apartment. When she reached for the door, her heart sank. It was ajar. She glanced down. A foot—Gramps's brown shoe—propped it open. Flashes of panic danced in her eyes while nausea roiled her gut.

She resisted the urge to force it open. She didn't want to hurt him. She crouched down and touched his ankle. "Gramps! Gramps!" she called. No answer.

She painstakingly pushed the door open a fraction and slammed her hip on the door handle as she stepped through the tight space. She slapped the switch and light illuminated the space inside the door.

Her grandfather lay on the floor, one leg bent at an awkward angle. Blood trickled from his head. Her mouth grew dry, and she struggled to form the words. "Gramps! Wake up." She held her breath and reached out with a shaky hand to feel for a pulse. Tears burned her eyes.

Please let there be a pulse. She hoped God listened to the prayers of hypocrites. She supposed her father was banking on it, so why couldn't she?

A *thrum-thrum-thrum* beat under her fingers.

Thank you.

"Gramps, Gramps, it's me. Gramps—" She shook him gently. Her mind blanked out on her CPR training. *A-B-Cs.* Something. Breathing. Something about breathing. She placed her hand on his chest. *Yes, he's breathing.* Pulse. Breathing. Two good signs. *What in the world does A-B-C stand for?*

Sarah plunked her purse down on the cracked tile and fished out her phone. The screen vibrated, rejecting her sweaty fingerprint. Frustrated, she jabbed in her password, then dialed 9-1-1.

She lifted her grandpa's head to rest on her thighs and she smoothed his mussed hair. "Help is on the way."

Please hurry.

CHAPTER 10

*a*n insistent vibration next to Sarah's hip pulled her out of a disjointed dream. She blinked a few times to get her bearings. She straightened her back and swiped a hand across the wet corner of her mouth and looked around the small hospital waiting room. A mother-daughter duo sat against the opposite wall, their eyes fixed on some early morning talk show. The happy chat grated on her nerves.

Sarah sat upright on the pleather couch, the horrific details of last night rising to the top of her consciousness. She reached into her purse, tucked between her hip and the arm of the couch and checked the time. *7:15.*

She had a missed call from Griff.

Her brow furrowed—she felt out of sorts struggling to remember what or where she had been heading before she found Gramps unconscious and bleeding by the alley door. Without checking her messages, she approached the administrator at the ER triage desk, half expecting her to bite Sarah's head off. Dealing with the public had to be a thankless job, especially when they were generally under duress. Instead, the woman was extremely pleasant. She assured

Sarah that nothing had changed with her grandfather and the doctors were awaiting his test results, and he'd be admitted to a room as soon as the day shift nurses got organized.

"Is he awake? Should I go back and keep him company?"

"He's sedated. He'll sleep for a few hours. If you leave your cell phone number, I can call you when he's moved," the woman offered. "Perhaps he'd want you to go home and rest." She smiled and tilted her chin toward the worn sofa. "Someplace other than here."

Sarah returned the woman's smile. She could only imagine how she looked, her head bobbing as she unsuccessfully fought off sleep. She rubbed the back of her neck. "Yeah, that wasn't the most comfortable place to sleep."

"Go home." The woman glanced at the computer monitor in front of her. "You're not far, right? I promise I'll call you once your father has been moved to a private room."

Sarah nodded, still not convinced she should leave, but the fogginess clamping down on her brain told her otherwise. She'd be good to no one if she couldn't think straight.

She barely remembered driving home. Before climbing out of her car, she grabbed her purse from the seat next to her and dug for the keys, cursing herself for not always slipping them in the easy-to-reach inside pocket. A knock on her car window made her jump. She looked up to find Griff haloed by the sun streaming in between the buildings.

She turned off the engine and the door locks released. As she unlatched the seat belt, he opened the door for her. He stepped back to give her some room as she climbed out.

"Everything okay?" he asked, a deep line furrowing his forehead.

Her words got lodged in her throat as she tried to process why he had been waiting for her in the alley. Did he have news about his niece? Hannah?

"You never met me at the diner," he said, answering her unasked question.

"I'm sorry." She shook her head in an attempt to snap out of her trance. "Last night...early this morning...I found Gramps unconscious in the entryway. When I got home." The throbbing behind her eyes indicated she was losing the battle with exhaustion. "He must have collapsed. They're running tests." For the first time since she had found Gramps, tears burned the back of her nose. She was not going to break down in front of this man again.

"What can I do?" His hand felt warm and solid on her lower back through her thin T-shirt.

She slid the key into the lock. "Nothing. He's resting and they're waiting to move him to a private room." Once inside, she paused at the bottom stair. "I should have called you." She wasn't used to relying on anyone other than Gramps. "I was—"

Griff reached out and softly brushed his thumb across her cheek. "No worries. Your grandfather takes priority."

"But your niece..." She clasped his hand and drew it away from her face. "And Hannah." With fatigue settling in her bones, she was ready to accept that Hannah was off living her best life somewhere. It certainly would make her life easier.

"Don't worry. Take care of your grandfather."

Sarah rubbed her eyes, then checked her fingers for mascara. "Did you get the posters up?"

"Yes. And the sheriff's department is now involved. We'll find her." She suspected his confident tone was for her benefit.

Sarah was about to say something reassuring—at least that's what her muddled brain thought she was about to do—when a voice called from the alley. "Hello?"

Griff pushed the door open, revealing Cailey, the young

waitress from the diner. "I saw your car, so I knew you were home. I wanted to make sure everyone was okay. Our night janitor saw an ambulance here."

"Gramps took a bad fall."

"Oh no, how is he? I love Russ. BLT light on the mayo." Cailey smiled after reciting his most frequent order. Technically, both hers and Gramps's favorite.

Her good humor was contagious, and a smile pulled at the corners of Sarah's mouth. "He's resting comfortably. Thanks for checking."

Cailey walked backward slowly. "Let me know when he's up for it. I'll make his favorite pie."

"Thank you." Some of the heaviness lifted from her heart. There were definitely perks to small-town living.

"Um…" Cailey seemed to be working something out in her mind. "Our night guy was kinda nosy. He overheard you talking to the EMT about how you found Gramps unconscious by the alley door."

A ticking started in Sarah's head again as she turned her full attention on the waitress. "Yeah."

"Well, if you want, the diner has a security camera on the door facing the alley."

Sarah waved her hand, automatically dismissing it. "He went out with his friends last night. He must have fallen when he arrived home. That's all."

"It couldn't hurt to take a look. I know Micky wouldn't mind." Cailey shrugged.

Griff touched Sarah's arm. "Can't hurt to look. You rest. I'll go." He jerked his chin toward the diner. "Is now okay?"

"Absolutely." Cailey looked like her day had just gotten a little more exciting.

Sarah shook her head. "No way, I'm coming with you." She pulled the door shut and checked the lock. "Let's go."

~

Griff and Sarah followed Cailey to the alley entrance to the diner. Only the vacant building separated their two businesses.

As the young waitress pushed the door open, she said, "I see you put flyers up this morning."

Griff's eyebrows drew up.

Cailey pressed her back against the door to hold it open. "I recognized the photo." Sarah, then Griff entered the small space. The smell of day-old grease assaulted his nose. "Besides, we don't have many people go missing here in Hunters Ridge. Well…" The waitress flicked Sarah a quick glance and her cheeks grew red. "Unless you count the Amish, but they mostly leave on their own."

Cailey waved her hand in dismissal, as if she was used to realizing she had said too much, yet she plowed on.

"We get a lot of traffic in this diner. If you have another copy, put it up in the front window."

Griff nodded. "I will. Thanks."

Cailey led them through the kitchen where a young man was scraping the grill with a metal spatula. "I'm sure you'll find her."

Griff pressed his lips together and nodded. He might be a number cruncher now, but much to his mother's chagrin, he had worked in the field when he first got out of Quantico. He had muttered that exact same sentiment more than once himself to a grief-stricken parent when their son or daughter went missing. The FBI didn't always find the victim, but in the moment, the words gave everyone a flicker of hope. Hadn't he done the same thing to his sister?

"Well," Cailey glanced toward the analog clock on the wall, "I have to get on the floor. The cloud keeps the video clips for five days. It's pretty straightforward if you want to download anything and send it to yourself." She seemed to study them both a minute. "You guys are tech savvy, right? Mick had me set everything up because he's hopeless..."

"We got it," Griff said. "We'll let you know when we're done."

"Sounds good." Cailey grabbed her apron from a hook by the door leading to the dining room. As she tied it around her waist, she said, "Let me at least get you started." She moved behind the desk and flopped down. The ancient office chair creaked and dipped back precariously. Undaunted, she grabbed the edge of the desk and pulled herself forward, the chair easily rolling on the worn linoleum. Her fingers flew across the keyboard. "I'll open the files." A series of video files appeared on the screen.

"Is it motion activated?" Griff asked.

"Yes." Cailey pointed to the screen. "See the time underneath each file?"

"I got home after three a.m.," Sarah said.

The buzzer sounded, indicating a customer had walked through the front door. "I think you've got it under control." Cailey smoothed a hand across her hair and checked her appearance in the small mirror by the door. "Let me know if you need anything."

Sarah took the seat Cailey had vacated. She discreetly wiped her palm down the thigh of her jeans, then placed it back on the mouse. The cursor slid across the bar advancing the timeframe, the light and shadows shifting in the alley. As deeper shadows cloaked the narrow space, lights popped on, circled in halos. A wave of anxiety swept over her as if she were reliving that night. An out-of-body experience of watching the event unfold. Unable to stop what was about to happen.

She released a shaky breath, trying to ease her nerves. Griff placed a comforting hand on her shoulder.

"Let's see, this is me coming home…" She was surprised at how businesslike she sounded when her insides were rioting.

Griff's arm brushed hers as he reached for the mouse. "May I?"

"Of course." Sarah tugged her hand away as if she might get burned, then immediately slouched in the chair trying to act all casual despite her gooey insides. She couldn't remember the last time her body had experienced such a strong physical reaction to a guy. She supposed it didn't matter how she felt, because mentally she'd never be prepared for a serious relationship.

Gee, he's just moving the mouse.

She focused intently on the screen and ignored the sheen of sweat that was probably glistening on her forehead. He clicked on another file. On the screen, the alley remained quiet. "I'm surprised the camera keeps coming on. I don't see anything."

"They're fairly sensitive. A bug can trigger it."

Sarah straightened and pressed her fingers into the small of her back. "Great. How many hours of bugs do we have to sort through?"

"Look there." Griff pointed at the monitor. Movement popped into the bottom right corner. There was something definitely there, but in this particular frame it was just dark shadows. A blob.

Even though Sarah knew the outcome of the events of that night, she couldn't stop the knots twisting in her stomach. Suddenly a slit of light spilled out into the alley. *Gramps.*

"There…" she whispered and leaned forward to study the

screen. Her grandfather limped while lugging a garbage bag. Funny, she hadn't noticed how pronounced his limp was. He disappeared, presumably to the dumpster.

Another dark shadow emerged from the corner of the video. Sarah leaned closer and her mouth grew dry. "Did you see that?"

"Yeah," Griff said. She sensed he was studying the screen as intently as she was.

The figure then darted toward the center of the frame, then disappeared in the direction of the hardware store's back door.

A cold chill raked down her spine. *Someone might have waited for him to take the garbage out. He does it every night without fail.* How many times had she told her clients who wanted to sneak away from their Amish life to mix up their schedules? Make it harder to be followed? Yet a person could set their watch by her grandpa's habits. Even though he had gone out with friends, he was home to take the garbage out at the same time. She could tell by the time stamp.

A few minutes later, Gramps headed back toward the alley door. Sarah covered her mouth, stifling a gasp. Gramps fell forward into the alley as someone ran out of the store.

Anger replaced her fear. *Who could do that?* Sarah's heart raced and dots danced in her line of vision. She blinked, trying to focus. Based on the rolling time stamp, three and a half minutes had elapsed while her grandfather took out the garbage. Someone had been in the building that entire time.

"It looks like he knew the placement of the camera," Griff said, his tone somber. "Or they got lucky."

"The person has something in their arms." She tapped the screen. "I can't see their face."

"The brim of his hat is perfectly angled."

The figure checked the alley. They set something down.

"It looks like papers." Her heart rate grew sluggish as realization dawned. "I think they're my files. From clients."

Sarah continued to watch in horror as they grabbed her grandfather's ankles and dragged him into the building.

Sarah's nerves buzzed like when she had too much caffeine, the cusp of an anxiety attack. She wiggled the mouse. She pushed back her chair, and without removing her eyes from the monitor she said, "Any way to zoom in on his face? Look." She leaned in closer. "He looks up for a fraction of a second. Maybe we can catch it. Can you do that? Do you know how?"

Griff planted his palm on the desk and pressed a few buttons on the keypad. The grainy image grew larger, but not any clearer. "It's pretty low quality. And the brim of his straw hat—is he Amish?" Disbelief edged his voice.

Sarah squinted. "If he's Amish, he's not married."

"How do you know?"

"No beard." Sarah rubbed the palm of her hand across her jaw. "Why would someone steal my files? Wait. Look at that." At the top of the screen, a group of people approached. They walked toward her grandfather's attacker. He seemed to tip his hat at them, but the group kept on walking.

"Wait, stop." Sarah's heart rate spiked. "Look, I know that guy. That's Hannah's brother."

"Hannah? The young Amish woman you're looking for?"

"One and the same." She crossed her arms and fisted her hands. "Timothy Shetler saw the man who attacked my grandfather." Her pulse thrummed loudly in her ears. "We have to go talk to him. *Now.*"

Guilt that someone had hurt Gramps in an effort to get to her files constricted like a band around her lungs, making it difficult to breathe. *Why?*

"Do you recognize the two other guys?"

"No, but I don't think they're Amish." Sarah stood and skirted past Griff. "Let's go ask him."

He pressed a few buttons to download the video and send it to his phone. They left through the dining room. Cailey was taking an order from an older couple in the corner booth. Other than that, the place was empty. Sarah waved and mouthed the words *Thank you*. She hoped they could leave without further discussion with the helpful—yet altogether too chatty—waitress.

Cailey lowered her pad and Sarah's heart sank. "Did you find what you needed?"

"Yes, thanks." Sarah wasn't about to go into detail in the middle of the dining room. "I'll brief you later."

"Come back for dinner. The special is meatloaf."

Sarah smiled. Her stomach growled, and she realized she hadn't eaten. At all. But it could wait. They had to find Timothy Shetler. He'd tell them the name of Gramps's attacker.

CHAPTER 11

*G*riff followed Sarah's instructions to park on the side of the road despite the wide—albeit muddy—driveway leading up to the Shetlers' farmhouse and barn. The sun was high in the sky and the fall morning was heavy with humidity. In the distance, a dark cloud promised a midday thunderstorm.

Sarah strode ahead of him, straight for the barn.

"Why not go to the house?" Griff called, straggling behind her and scanning the property.

Sarah shook her head and placed a single finger to her lips. "We want to talk to Timothy without Mr. Shetler around. He shows up, game over." She had warned Griff in the truck on the way over that Timothy would get squirrelly if he thought they were accusing him of something improper. And if Mr. Shetler found her on his property, he'd run them off.

Griff didn't know much about the Amish, but apparently, they weren't immune to the same types of drama that plagued the rest of the world.

An earthy smell reached Griff's nose. It wasn't awful. Just

different. He was more familiar with the aromas from pizza, rotting garbage, and exhaust fumes that sprang up and surprised a person on a busy city street.

Sarah slowed at the barn door. She glanced over her shoulder, her eyebrows raised. A brightness shone in her eyes as if she had struck pay dirt. "Timothy's mucking the stalls. Alone. Come on."

When they approached Timothy, he stopped mid-shovel. His gaze moved behind them toward the door. "What do you want?" He spat out the question.

Sarah held up her hand. "We—"

"My *dat* sent you away." Timothy cut her off and pivoted on his heel. He scooped up another pile and dumped it into a steel bucket. "Go before you cause me a hassle."

"I need a few answers first," Sarah said.

"Hah." Timothy continued his chores, as if ignoring them would make them disappear.

"It'll only take a minute," Sarah said, pleading. "This is my friend Griff. His niece is missing, and we're worried she and your sister are together." She stopped short of telling him they had both called Mr. Gilmore for a ride prior to going off the radar.

Timothy turned to face them and jabbed the earth with the pitchfork. He rested his elbow on its handle. "My sister left. What she does is not my business."

"Is that how you repay her?" Sarah asked, stepping forward.

Timothy blanched, recovered quickly, and glared at her harshly. "Go away."

Griff watched the exchange. *I wonder what that's all about?*

Timothy set the pitchfork against the wall and took off his straw hat. "I'm getting married in a week. You're going to ruin everything."

"I'm not looking to interfere with your life," Sarah said,

barely above a whisper. "You were in the alley last night behind the hardware store."

The young Amish man's eyes grew round, then narrowed, as a lie—no doubt—died on his lips. Griff had seen this reaction many times in his line of work. The urge to lie was strong when you were caught dead to rights.

"Stop before you say anything else. We have video of you." Sarah had lost the cordial tone and pinned him with a steely gaze Griff made a mental note to avoid.

Timothy palmed the top of his hat and shoved it down farther on his head, finally the full impact of Sarah's intensity settling on him. He wasn't going to be able to talk his way out of this. Griff had mistakenly assumed a young Amish man would be more amiable, but he supposed people were people. And Timothy obviously had something to hide.

"You passed someone standing in the alley. You spoke to him. I'm not sure if he was Amish, but he did have on a straw hat and a large field coat even though it was warm out."

Timothy's eyes darted around the barn, as if planning his escape. "I was there." A defiance edged his voice. "I went out with my buddies. We had a few beers. We took a shortcut through the alley."

"Who are your friends? They didn't look Amish."

"Who said I couldn't have *Englisch* friends?" He shrugged. "I won't be seeing them much once I get hitched."

"I don't care who your friends are, unless I need them to give me the information you won't." Sarah crossed her arms and rocked back on her heels. "Who was in the alley behind the hardware store last night?"

He lowered his gaze and pushed some hay around on the ground with his worn boot.

"Tell me."

"I don't remember. I was drunk."

"I don't believe you." Griff spoke up for the first time.

Timothy smirked. "I don't even know you."

Sarah introduced them and when Timothy heard FBI agent, he shot her a "you've got to be kidding me" look. "I went out for a few drinks. Period. I'm sure the bishop wouldn't be thrilled, but I didn't realize it was a federal offense." His choice of words suggested he had spent time outside his community during what Sarah had called *Rumspringa.*

Sarah glanced toward the barn door. "Maybe I should say hello to your dad before I leave. Maybe I should tell him I saw you out drinking last night."

"You wouldn't."

Sarah shrugged.

Timothy slowly crossed his arms and settled in with a smug expression on his face. "*Neh*, I call your bull. You'll lose the trust of the Amish girls looking to jump the fence if you go running to one of their *dats.* Won't you?"

"I don't have time for this nonsense." Sarah huffed. "Your sister did you a solid. She took blame for Emma Mae's suitcase. Maybe your *dat* would like to hear about that."

"*Neh.*" Timothy took off his hat and scratched his head. "I saw Elmer Graber in the alley last night."

"What?" Shock rounded Sarah's eyes. "Elmer?"

"*Yah.*" Timothy seemed more fidgety now that he had given them a name. "But I'm not going to repeat that to the sheriff or anything." He puffed up his chest, growing insolent again. "I'll deny it. We"—Griff assumed, easily so, that *we* meant the Amish—"don't care much for law enforcement. I don't want trouble. I'm getting married."

Sarah studied him for a long moment. "If I find out you're lying, I'll be back." She turned to leave.

Griff hovered over Timothy in an effort to intimidate. He wasn't proud of it, but sometimes he had to do what he had to do. Perhaps these events were all related to his niece's disappearance. Or maybe they weren't. But his growing fondness for Sarah made him want to help her regardless. "Are you telling the truth?" He knew next to nothing about the Amish, but he was adept at reading body language.

The mutinous set of Timothy's eyes suggested he'd sooner impale Griff with a pitchfork than admit anything.

~

Sarah climbed into Griff's truck and slammed the door harder than she had intended. She scratched angrily at a fresh mosquito bite. "I don't believe it." She slumped into the passenger seat. "We're on a wild goose chase." She punched the door with the side of her fist, then hugged it to her chest. *Stupid.* "I should be at the hospital with Gramps."

"I'll take you there and then follow up with this Graber kid."

"No, he's Amish with a lot of backstory. You won't get anywhere with him or his family. Last I heard, he was on probation."

Griff's eyes widened. "An Amish guy on probation?"

"He harassed a woman he blamed for his sister's death." Sarah pressed a fingernail into the mosquito bite, hoping that would distract her from the annoying itch. "Elmer's sister, Abby, worked for one of the wealthy families in town." She dropped her hand to her lap. "You ever notice the large home up on the hill?"

"It caught my eye. I figured someone who had a lot of money didn't want neighbors."

"Well, Abby, Elmer's sister, worked for the family, and she and the owner's daughter became friends. When Violet left to work for her mother in New York City, Abby went with her. It was a big deal because she also left her Amish faith.

Sadly, she was murdered in Violet's New York City apartment."

Griff muttered something Sarah didn't quite catch.

"Elmer blamed Violet and ran her off the road. He got pretty banged up in the process. He's lucky to be alive and on probation, not in jail."

"Do you think Timothy was lying to cover for someone else?"

Sarah shrugged. "I think throwing Elmer under the bus is convenient. He's the perfect scapegoat."

"Why does Timothy owe his sister?" Griff asked.

Sarah shared how Hannah had taken the blame for a suitcase full of clothes in the barn that had been Timothy's fiancée's. Emma Mae and Timothy had planned to run away and get married but changed their minds and decided to stay and rush their marriage to hide their indiscretion. They had already been baptized and were awaiting their wedding which just so happened to be next week. But Sarah felt all this information was peripheral to what they were working on, and she didn't want Timothy's future wife to suffer further embarrassment if word got out.

Warm anger spread to her limbs at the injustice of it. Emma Mae would suffer the brunt of the shunning if their secret got out. But she hadn't gotten pregnant by herself.

"Is that it?" Griff asked.

"That's a pretty big deal around here."

"So should we go to this guy's house? See if there's anything to what Timothy's saying?"

Sarah bit her lower lip. "Yes, we have to." Her phone vibrated in her purse. She lifted a finger. "Hold on."

Sarah glanced at the display. *Chrissy, a nurse at the hospital.* She immediately started beating herself up. She should be with Gramps, not running around town with a man she had only met. But she knew Gramps was being well cared for and she couldn't shake the gut feeling that Hannah—and Griff's niece—had found themselves in trouble. The big questions were: Were they together? And if so, where? And was the incident at the hardware store related?

"Hello. I wanted to give you an update on Gramps." Fortunately, the nurse on duty was a longtime friend of Sarah's. Many of her close friends had gotten into the habit of calling her grandfather by his nickname. He seemed to love it.

"How is he?" Sarah pointed to the road, indicating Griff should get a move on. Without waiting for an answer, she added, "I'm on my way to the hospital right now." They'd follow up with Elmer later.

Griff got the hint and shifted the truck into Drive.

"That's good, because he's asking for you."

Sarah's heart leapt. "He's awake?"

"He woke up about ten minutes ago. The doctor did a quick assessment, and she's ordered a few more tests, but he's stable and he's asking for you."

Thank God.

"Has he said anything about what happened?"

"Not that I know of." The hustle and bustle in the background seemed to distract her friend.

"I'll be there in five minutes."

"Great, he'll be happy to see you."

"And Chrissy, thanks for looking after him."

"Happy to, sweetie." Before Sarah had a chance to say anything more, Chrissy added, "Make sure you're not burning the candle at both ends. Gramps is going to need you. It'll be a long recovery."

Another pang of guilt sucker punched her. She hadn't even considered opening the store today. But they couldn't afford to stay closed and lose customers. Gramps would get agitated once he found out.

"See you in a few." Sarah ended the call.

"Everything okay?" The warmth in Griff's voice touched her heart. It seemed like they had known each other for a lot longer than a few days. But perhaps their shared concern led to a forced intimacy that would evaporate once the girls were found safe.

Please let the girls be found safe.

"I'll make some phone calls while you visit your grandfather." Griff slowed inside the front lobby of the hospital.

"Um…" Sarah had expected him to come to the room, but he obviously had things to do. He said he was going to call his associate in the FBI and see if anything came up on Nicholas Gilmore, or if he had any success accessing Lexi's smartphone. "If you need to leave, just text me. I'll find my own way home," Sarah said.

"Okay."

Her heart dropped a little. Selfishly, she had hoped he'd insist on waiting.

When she reached her grandfather's room, he was sleeping. She quietly lowered herself into a vinyl-cushioned chair and took comfort in the steady rise and fall of his chest. He looked frail under the white hospital blanket. She slumped into the chair and closed her eyes. She'd rest for just a minute.

"And they said *I* needed rest." Her grandpa's scratchy voice startled her. She bolted upright.

"Gramps…" She jumped up and swayed a moment. She placed a hand on the rail of his bed to steady herself. "How are you feeling?" She kissed his forehead.

"Fine." He leaned forward awkwardly, as if to conspire with her. "You've got to get me out of here."

"Chrissy assured me that it wouldn't be long. Maybe a few more days."

A corner of his mouth hitched up. "Days?" He shook his head. "I have to open the hardware store."

Again, that pang of guilt. "I'm sorry, I should have made keeping it open a priority."

Gramps waved his hand. His fingers seemed thinner, frailer. "I can't expect you to run it. You have your own job. And last I checked, you had a few other things going on." He looked past her toward the door. "Did that gentleman find his niece?"

"Not yet. We're working together on that. I'm worried…" She let her words trail off. She didn't want to burden Gramps with her problems while he recuperated.

"I hope you didn't call your mother."

Sarah jerked her head back. She hadn't spoken to her mother or father in years. Heat crept up her face. "I'm sorry. I probably should have done that, too." Had she become that insensitive? Her mother was Gramps's daughter. Didn't she deserve to know her dad was injured?

"Don't you dare." Gramps's eyes flared wide. "They don't need to know anything about this. That son-in-law of mine will be selling the hardware store and sticking me in an old folks home. Nope, don't tell them. I just had a little spill. Nothing to call the troops in for."

Sarah furrowed her brow. "Do you remember what happened?"

"You mean how I ended up here?" He lifted a shaky hand to touch the bandage on his head. "I tripped while taking the garbage out."

Sarah rested her hip on the edge of the bed and scratched her neck, turning away from her grandfather.

"Oh, Sarah, you've never been very good at hiding things from me."

She gently squeezed Gramps's hand. "Griff and I watched the surveillance camera the diner has set up in the alley."

"Is my fall going to make *Funniest Home Videos?*" Gramps waggled his eyebrows.

"Someone attacked you."

Confusion narrowed his eyes. "I don't remember that." His cheek twitched. "You'd think I'd remember that."

"You've had a head injury. We can talk to the doctor and find out when you'll regain your memories." She lifted his hand and kissed it. "What's important is that you're okay."

Gramps gingerly touched the back of his hand. "You gotta get me sprung."

"We need to make sure you're okay first."

"The food in here is garbage." Gramps frowned and made a big show of shuddering.

"You couldn't have had much to eat. You've been sleeping most of the time." A bruise on the side of his face had turned an angry shade of purple. "I'm not going to take you home until the doctor gives us the okay." Sarah stood and adjusted the hem of her shirt over her jeans. "You rest. I'll jot down my cell phone number if you need anything." She touched the handset of the landline on the small table.

"I'll rest if you bring me a BLT from the diner."

"You got it!" She started to leave, then turned back around. "I love you."

"Don't be getting all dramatic on me. I'm fine."

"I know." She swallowed around a lump of emotion.

Sarah was almost out of earshot when she heard Gramps holler, "Love you too, kiddo."

CHAPTER 12

"*I* called the sheriff's department." Griff had no choice after seeing the surveillance video. "They'll send someone to the Grabers' house to check on Elmer when they get a chance." Griff drummed his fingers on the steering wheel of his truck as he headed out of the hospital parking lot. "When they get a chance," he repeated in disbelief. "Apparently they're short-staffed. The sheriff isn't even around. Something about a fishing trip. I mentioned Elmer was on parole, so maybe that will light a fire under them."

"Thank you." Sarah seemed so much lighter since she had spoken to her grandfather. The medical staff had assured her that he'd make a full recovery despite his compromised memory. Poor guy slammed his head pretty hard.

"Did the sheriff's department have any updates on Lexi?" She adjusted the AC vents on his dash.

"Unfortunately, no. But at least they're looking for her now." He hated that it had come to this. He truly thought he'd drive to Hunters Ridge on Monday, find his niece, and bring her—reluctantly—home.

"How is that going to go over with your sister?"

Griff had told Sarah how Jeannie was in a custody battle with her ex over their youngest daughters. "At this point, my sister's sole focus is on bringing Lexi home safe. I think she'd hand over her daughters to her ex if it meant having her oldest daughter home. Safe." He sighed heavily. "I'm really worried."

"I'm sorry if all this other stuff is a distraction." Her compassionate tone touched his heart.

He shook his head. "My gut tells me these events are related. Well...at least Hannah and Lexi. This Nicky kid is up to no good."

"Then let's go shake the tree again," Sarah said. "I know him. He gets chatty when he's nervous. That's how he was as a kid."

Griff didn't need to be asked twice. He made a wide U-turn on the country road and gunned his truck toward the Gilmores' home. Dark rain clouds made it seem later than it was. When he pulled up the driveway, the white van sat in the same spot. "Wonder why Chester Gilmore hasn't called me."

"It's strange." Sarah's voice had a faraway quality to it.

Griff pushed open the door and glanced at her over his shoulder. "Wait here." The Gilmore house was quiet except for a curtain fluttering in one of the open upstairs windows.

Sarah shook her head. "I'm going with you. I know Nick. If he's going to talk, he'll talk to me."

Griff nodded, but wasn't happy about it. He couldn't figure out why he felt so protective of Sarah in such a short time. Or maybe it was because of his job—he was protective of the public by nature. But Sarah was more than that...

He shook aside the distracting thought and strode toward the front door, guiding Sarah with a hand to the small of her back. After a few repeated knocks, it was pretty obvious no one was going to answer.

"Maybe he fell asleep watching TV," she suggested.

"Or he's ignoring us. I wonder where his dad is." He took a step off the porch and stared up at the open window. Thunder rumbled in the distance. He jerked his head toward the side. "I have an idea."

Sarah followed him, her tennis shoes sucking into the damp earth under the long grass. "Where are we going?" She spoke in hushed tones.

"The barn. I've wanted to check it out since the first time I came out here."

"Don't you need a warrant or something?" Sarah asked, picking up her pace and glancing over her shoulder as if they were about to be caught.

"Forget about rules. My niece's well-being is more important than a piece of paper." He'd deal with the consequences after he found his niece. The ground grew softer the deeper they got into the yard. He slowed. "You want to wait in the truck?"

"No way."

His heart raced, not from the exertion, but from the possibility of gaining access to the barn. He glanced over his shoulder. The back of the house remained quiet. *Ten more feet.* He wasn't sure why he felt compelled to check out its contents. A squirrelly kid like Nick could be stashing anything in there. Weapons. Drugs. *My niece.*

A knot formed between Griff's shoulder blades when he reached the barn. He examined the structure. Old, but someone had painted the brittle wood at least once in his lifetime. The doors were padlocked. Griff's pulse spiked. Who padlocked an old barn? He supposed there could be any number of legitimate reasons—equipment, discouraging trespassers—but he had to get in there to make sure.

He yanked on the lock, then turned it over in his hands. It was rusted shut. He pulled again, hoping maybe a link in the chain was weak. No luck.

"Hannah!" Sarah called, speaking for the first time. "Hannah." They both stood still, their exerted breaths mingled with the crickets.

Anxious anticipation bubbled up in his stomach. He leaned toward the door and hollered, "Lexi! Lexi." He held his breath, waiting for an answer.

Nothing. *Why did I think she was here?*

He couldn't stop until he got inside. What if she was unconscious? Or maybe he was letting his thoughts run away from him. Maybe he *had* been sitting behind a desk for too long. Maybe his field instincts were off.

"I don't think anyone is here," Sarah said, rolling up on the balls of her sneakers and planting her hands on the wood. She peered through the narrow openings between the wooden boards. "I can't see anything."

He held up his finger in a hold-on-a-minute gesture and strolled the perimeter, searching for another way in. Along the way, he studied the ground. No sign of fresh tracks other than from small animals. Griff found a rusted crowbar partially obscured by the long grass. He picked it up and jogged toward the doors.

"This might work."

Sarah took a step back.

He slid the bar behind the lock, gained leverage against the dried wood and forced the crowbar down. The chain snapped with one quick crank of the bar and fell to the hard-packed earth like a clanking snake. He peeled back the door, its hinges emitting a high-pitched groan. The smell of damp hay hit his nostrils. "Lexi," he called again.

"Hannah!" Sarah yelled.

A cloud of dust and stale hay swirled in the air. An old

tractor with metal wheels sat in the far corner. Rusted tools hung on the walls. A Chevy Chevette from the eighties was partially obscured by bales of hay.

"I need to check the loft," Griff said, dragging a ladder over to it. "Steady this. I'm going up."

≈

Sarah's pulse rioted in her throat. She could envision a rung snapping and sending Griff down into a heap of broken bones.

Fortunately, Griff must have had the same vision because he grabbed both sides of the ladder, checked that it was steady against the edge of the loft, then proceeded slowly, checking his weight on each rung.

"You think this is a good idea?" She scooted behind him and held the ladder in place, doubting she'd truly be of any help if this thing went sideways. "This ladder is ancient. It might not hold you."

"I'll be fine."

Famous last words.

She tipped her head back to watch Griff climb higher and higher, her grip on the rough wood growing tighter and tighter. At the top, he dug his phone out and flashed the light in the space. He muttered his annoyance under his breath.

"Anything?" She glanced toward the barn door, expecting company at any minute.

Griff started to back down, and the ladder shifted under his weight but remained secure. "Not if you count cobwebs and something small and fuzzy in the corner."

"At least now you know there's nothing here," Sarah added, trying to force a cheeriness in a dismal situation. What she wouldn't give to know his niece and Hannah were safe, allowing her to go home, shower and crawl into bed to sleep. For days.

Well, after taking care of Gramps.

Griff neared the bottom of the ladder, then jumped down to the hard earth of the barn. He dragged his palms together. "I'm out of ideas. Lexi would never disappear for this long. Maybe she's no longer in Hunters Ridge." His tone held dark edges. Perhaps his mind was toying with the worst-case scenario.

The sound of overgrown grass being disturbed grew closer. Griff squinted toward the light coming in near the open barn door, concern etched on his face. Sarah's heart leapt as he reached for his gun.

Deputy Caitlin Flagler stood in the doorway, gun in hand.

Griff lifted his hands. "Special Agent Trevor Griffin with the FBI. We met in town."

The deputy groaned and then relaxed her posture and holstered her gun. "What are you doing here?"

"I needed to check out this building. Did Nick call you?"

The deputy adjusted her hat a fraction and answered vaguely. "I got a call about a possible trespasser." Her gaze drifted from Griff to Sarah and back. "Trespassers." She emphasized the *s*.

"It's just us," Sarah said.

"You two are keeping me hopping. I was headed to the Grabers' place when I got this call." Deputy Flagler entered the barn, her gaze alert. "Find anything?"

"Not unless you count this Chevy classic."

The deputy smirked. "I don't think anyone would consider the Chevette as a classic."

"Sorry, Deputy Flagler, we're just trying to find my niece. And Hannah."

The deputy smiled at Sarah. "Please, call me Caitlin, especially since we're going to keep running into each other like this."

"Are you the only one on duty?" Griff asked.

"We're short-staffed."

"I was sorry to hear Olivia was laid up," Sarah said.

"So is she. She doesn't do rest well." Caitlin tipped her head toward the door. "Let's get out of here before Nick blows a gasket. I'm gonna make a show of coming down hard on you both. And when we get to the driveway, don't waste time leaving, okay?"

Sarah was relieved they weren't going to get arrested. That was the last thing she needed. She pointed toward the house. "Any chance we can talk to Chester Gilmore? His van's home, so I'm going to assume he is, too."

"Let's give it a try." Caitlin led the way back to the house.

Nick was sitting on the porch steps when they reached the driveway. He was sucking on a cigarette. He drew in a deep breath and let it out, not seeming to be in a hurry. "I want to press charges for trespassing."

Caitlin stood over him, asserting her authority. "Now, you don't want to make me have to fill out all that paper-work, do you, Nicky?"

The young man looked up at her, a hint of hesitation flashing in his eyes. "They *were* trespassing."

"Maybe they were taking a walk and got lost."

Nicky's lips pursed. "They were trespassing."

"Nicholas, you and I have a pretty good relationship, right?"

The kid stubbed out his cigarette on the porch and muttered something Sarah couldn't make out, but he wasn't happy. No doubt Nicky had run-ins with the law. Rumor had it that he got more than a few breaks from the sheriff's department.

"Why don't we just let Ms. James and Agent Griffin be on

their way? No harm, no foul." When Nick didn't answer, Caitlin added, "Sound good?"

Nicky grabbed onto the railing and stood. "Stay away from my house."

He started to go into the house when Caitlin said, "Send your dad out. I'd like to say hello."

Nicky froze before turning around. His gaze drifted to the van sitting in the driveway, then back to the people standing in front of him. "He went out with a friend. He doesn't carry a cell phone," he quickly added.

Caitlin adjusted her stance, seeming to weigh her response. "Do me a favor, then. Have him call me as soon as he gets back, okay?"

Nicky shrugged and turned to leave. He slammed the inside door and Sarah could sense him watching them from the window.

They walked over to Griff's truck. "Thanks for not dragging us down to the sheriff's station."

Caitlin smiled. "No problem." She gestured toward the house with her chin. "Anything we need to explore?"

"No." Griff pulled open the door to his truck. "Something about this kid…"

"You're not wrong. He's been in trouble before, but until you can prove he's got something to do with your niece's disappearance, you have to stop coming out here," Caitlin said. "Oh, and about Elmer. I called his parole officer. He has an ankle monitor."

Sarah shook her head. "How do they work out the logistics on a farm without electricity?"

"They have models that run off cell towers." The deputy patted the door, as if she was going to leave, then she turned back. "Any reason Elmer would want to attack your grandfather?"

Sarah's stomach pitched. "A witness said he saw him in the alley at the time Gramps was attacked."

Caitlin pondered this for a moment. "Crime of opportunity? Russ was in the wrong place at the wrong time?"

"Elmer may have thought I had something to do with his sister leaving Hunters Ridge."

Caitlin held out her hand. "Did you?"

"No, but maybe he knows about my work with other Amish women." Sarah didn't bother to hold back. After the fiasco this past summer, the secret was out. "Maybe he doesn't want me to help anyone else." She shrugged. "Whoever hurt my grandfather also stole the files from my office."

"Did you check the cameras in the area?" Caitlin tapped her chin with her index finger.

"The diner has one facing the alley," Sarah said. "That's how we ID'd our witness."

"The attacker's face was obscured by a straw hat," Griff added.

"Doesn't exactly narrow things down around here." Caitlin tipped her hat toward her patrol car. "Let me show you how high-tech Hunters Ridge is."

She climbed behind the steering wheel, leaving the door open, and pivoted her laptop so they could see the screen. Heat radiated off Griff's body as he trapped Sarah between him and the open door.

Caitlin pressed a few keys. "What time are we looking at here?"

"Early this morning." Sarah gave Caitlin the time they spotted Timothy Shetler.

"Okay, there are two exit points from that alley." Caitlin clicked a few more keys. She pulled one up. She hit play on the feed and there was nothing. Not even a bug. Then she clicked on the other one, shortly after the time the intruder with the straw hat barged out of the hardware store.

Sarah rolled back on her heels and gasped. Griff bracketed her forearms from behind, steadying her.

Caitlin paused on the image. "It's the right time."

Sarah nodded. A lone person stepped out onto the street, empty-handed. "But it's not Elmer," she whispered as a buzzing drowned out everything around her.

"Do you know that person?" Griff's deep voice washed over the back of her neck. Goose bumps raced across Sarah's exposed skin as her mind tried to process what she was seeing.

"Yes. It's Emma Mae. She's engaged to Timothy Shetler. Why did she attack my grandfather?" Sarah fought hard to maintain her composure. She inched closer and stretched her arm across Caitlin to point at the screen. "And what did she do with my files?"

CHAPTER 13

"*A*re you sure?" Caitlin asked, her face lit up by the bluish glow of her laptop screen inside her patrol car. The autumn air was ripe with an impending thunderstorm.

"Yes, I'm sure." Sarah stepped back, right into Griff, then sidestepped away from him. She needed room, air.

"I'll go pick her up. Question her," Caitlin said.

Sarah's mind raced. She wanted justice for her grandfather, but her heart also broke for the young Shetler boys who had experienced so much loss of late. Emma Mae had slipped in and taken over after Hannah left. And her wedding to Timothy was next week. "Can it wait?" Her question came more from empathy than practicality.

"Why?" Caitlin snapped the laptop closed. "We need to ask her what she was doing coming out of the alley seconds after someone knocked your grandfather over. He was seriously injured."

"I know." Sarah tapped her lips with the tips of her fingers, struggling to make sense of her emotions. She also had information the deputy didn't. Hannah had gone to great lengths to protect a secret. But bringing Emma Mae in for questioning now would only blow up all their plans. "Emma Mae is getting married to Timothy Shetler next week."

"We can't overlook this," Caitlin said. "She was there."

Griff placed a hand on her shoulder. "She's a witness, at least."

Sarah glanced up at Griff. "It wouldn't matter. Witness or perpetrator, being out in that alley late at night would be a major transgression. That would explain why Timothy lied. He knew it was Emma Mae."

"But didn't you see a guy leaving the back of the hardware store?"

"He was slight," Griff said. "Easy for a woman to throw on an oversize coat and hat."

"Let me bring her in. We'll get to the bottom of this," Caitlin said.

"Please let me do some digging first. I don't believe Emma Mae will cause any more problems. She was after something specific." Sarah was beginning to put the puzzle pieces together. If she was right.

"Okay," Caitlin sighed, "I'm not a fan of trying to deal with the Amish anyway. It's always a headache. For a group who's all about God, they certainly have their share of secrets." She climbed out of the patrol car and looped her thumbs through her utility belt.

Sarah didn't miss the edge to the deputy's tone. She understood. Trying to live the tenets of the Amish faith—and the severe consequences if one didn't—made it ripe for secrecy.

"Thank you." Sarah scanned the house one last time and made eye contact with Nicky in the kitchen window, watching them. She didn't have to wonder why he was avoiding her. Sarah suspected she was one of the few people outside his family who knew *his* childhood secrets.

"In the meantime," Caitlin said, "stay off this property. And don't stir things up with the Amish. I don't feel like chasing my tail, okay? I've got more than I can handle in this town until the sheriff can loosen some purse strings and hire a few more deputies."

"Okay," Sarah said, already thinking ahead to the conversation she was going to have with Emma Mae. *What had she been doing?*

~

Sarah delivered Gramps a BLT sandwich at the hospital and then both she and Griff headed back to the hardware store. The physician told her Gramps needed a few more days. But based on his familiar wit and his pink color, she suspected he'd be home before long.

But what would he be coming home to? Every time she drove up to the hardware store, the *Closed* sign dangling in the window made the guilt twist in her gut. She might feel less guilty if she didn't feel like she was spinning her wheels all day.

But *were* they really spinning their wheels? They had learned Emma Mae had been in the alley and Timothy Shetler had lied about it. As much as she wanted to like the two, their selfishness and secrecy were wasting her time.

And it almost cost her the person she loved most. Sarah could only speculate that Emma Mae had surprised her grandfather and either pushed him over or he fell, the result being the same. But Sarah and Griff had decided to do a little more digging before confronting Emma Mae who would most likely lie, like her fiancé had.

Another idea whispered across her brain. *Did Timothy put her up to it?* It still didn't explain why.

Sarah turned the key in the lock in the alley door, then

paused with her hand on the knob. "If Emma Mae ran out the back of the hardware store and then emerged on Main Street back in her plain clothes, she had to drop the straw hat and man's coat somewhere."

And the files...

"There's a trash bin in the alley and it won't be emptied until tomorrow morning." Sarah met Griff's gaze. The light bulb above the door reflected in his eyes.

"Let's go check." Thunder rumbled in the distance. The storm had skirted the town.

"I'll grab a flashlight."

When she returned, they headed straight for the trash in the narrow alley that ran between the buildings and dumped onto Main Street.

Sarah flicked on the flashlight. The beam of light landed on the side of the dumpster. She pretended not to see something scurry behind it but her entire body shuddered.

Using both hands, she pushed up the lid of the large garbage bin. She stumbled back. "Oh, yuck." The words were muffled behind the crook of her elbow covering her mouth and nose. The pungent smell nearly made her gag. "I can't…" This wasn't the feminist mountain she wanted to die on.

"Need my help?" Humor laced his voice.

She nodded vigorously, her nose and mouth still firmly tucked into the crook of her arm.

Griff stepped up beside her, his stomach heaving at the strong stench. A handful of flies buzzed the surface of the garbage. "Nasty."

"Yep." She aimed the flashlight into the opening and seemed to be conserving words, or maybe it was her breath she was holding.

The top layer consisted primarily of black bags of garbage, a few with tears in their thick plastic, their contents made more putrid from age and heat. He reached in and grabbed the first bag and placed it outside the dumpster. He continued until the loose items on the bottom of the dumpster became visible, including a straw hat, a farm coat, and a slew of paper, not to mention the various detritus that belonged on the bottom of the dumpster.

What is that brown stuff? His stomach grew queasy when he realized he'd have to hop in if he hoped to retrieve those papers.

He studied Sarah's watering eyes above her arm. Despite the messy job ahead of him, he felt a smile pulling at the corners of his mouth. He stifled a chuckle. "Any chance you can see what's on those papers down there before I jump in?"

Her chest filled with air and she exhaled heavily. She stepped to the edge of the dumpster and looked in. She flashed the beam of light around and stepped back suddenly, dry heaving. Once she calmed down, she said, "Oh man, I'm sorry. I am so squeamish."

"No problem. It's pretty ripe." He glanced down at his jeans and sneakers and figured he'd probably have to burn them after this. "Could you make anything out?"

She nodded. "My handwriting."

"I guess I'm going for a dumpster dive." His stomach threatened to revolt.

"Really?" The single word sounded apologetic and appreciative and maybe a little doubtful all at the same time.

"I'm thirty-one, not ninety-one. I've got this." Without waiting another beat, he grabbed the edge of the garbage bin and hoisted himself up and in. He landed hard and his right heel slid out for a second before gaining purchase. He could only imagine what he had just smooshed. He cleared his throat and took shallow breaths through his mouth.

"Aim the light here." He tossed the straw hat and coat out. Then he plucked out the papers, some relatively clean, others smeared with...he didn't even want to think about it. He stood up and pointed to one of the cardboard boxes stacked next to the bin, probably someone's half-hearted idea of recycling since it technically wasn't mixed in among the garbage, but it clearly hadn't been placed in the recycling bin that was located elsewhere. "Grab one of those boxes. I'll drop the papers into it."

Sarah jogged over and snagged a box. She held it up. A gust of wind swept a long dark strand of hair across her face, but she didn't have a free hand to tug it away. If his hands were clean—and if he knew her better—he would have hooked his finger around it and pulled it away from her face, but it felt like the gesture might have been too intimate.

Griff picked up each piece of paper and tossed it into the box. After a few minutes, he turned around in the confined space and tossed a few bags aside to make sure he didn't miss any papers. "I got it all, as far as I can tell."

Sarah set the box down and it landed with a thwack. "Need a hand?" She backed up, assessing the situation.

"I wouldn't be much of an FBI agent if I couldn't find my way out of a dumpster."

Sarah tilted her head, as if to say, *Suit yourself.*

He grabbed the edge and hoisted himself out, much as he had gotten in. He didn't want to touch anything. *Anything else.* Not until he washed his hands. Sarah picked up the box. Griff didn't offer to help for two reasons: his hands were dirty, and he had a strong sense she'd take offense. Sarah was fiercely independent until it came to climbing into dumpsters.

He couldn't blame her.

Sarah balanced the box on one hip and opened the back

door to the hardware store. She held it open with her backside. "Bathroom to your right."

Griff washed his hands, and when he came out Sarah seemed to be studying him. "You can't get in your car. You'll never get the stink out."

Griff laughed. "I don't believe I've ever had anyone say that to me before." Never mind a beautiful woman.

"No, seriously." She bit her lower lip, as if considering. "I wish I had clean clothes to offer you." She pointed up. "My grandpa and I live in an apartment upstairs. I do have a shower, but there's no point if you don't have fresh clothes."

He glanced down. A brown and yellow smudge marred the front of his shirt. *Oh, man.* Part of being a desk jockey meant he never had to change his pants midshift. *Ugh.* "I do have another change of clothes in a duffel bag in my trunk. I had checked out of the motel, hoping I'd find Lexi and we could go home today." He realized how unrealistically hopeful he had been early this morning. He studied her for a brief moment. "If you don't mind. I'd love to get out of these nasty clothes."

"Please, yes. It's the least I can do. Hold on." She put the box down on the office floor and pushed it deeper in with the foot of her shoe, then held out her hand. "Give me your car keys. I'll get your bag."

To the right was a flight of stairs, presumably leading to the apartment.

"Here's my keys. The green one opens the apartment. Go help yourself. Clean towels and whatever you might need are in the linen closet just outside the bathroom. Place is pretty small. I'm sure you'll find it." She held up her index finger before he could protest. "I'll be right back with your clothes."

~

Heat crept up Sarah's cheeks, wondering how she had ended up here, standing outside her own bathroom, frozen with a man's clothes. A man she hardly knew. Finally, she cleared her throat and squared her shoulders and knocked, two raps in quick succession. Very businesslike. Inwardly she groaned. There was nothing businesslike about any of this.

Figuring he couldn't hear the knocks, she squeezed her eyes shut and opened the door a crack. "I'm going to slide your duffel bag on the floor." She smiled to herself. She sounded like someone handling hostage negotiations. *Come out with your dirty clothes and no one gets hurt.*

She heard rather than saw the crinkling of the shower liner. "Thanks."

Keeping her head down, she opened her eyes. His dirty clothes were on a pile in the center of the tile floor. She quickly gathered them up. Steam rose from around the shower curtain. She backed out of the bathroom and closed the door.

With her one free hand, she pulled open the shuttered doors on the far end of the small apartment. She did a quick check of his pockets, then tossed his clothes in the washer, hoping he didn't mind that she had thrown everything in together. The agitator kicked in, she added detergent, and she figured it was too late to ask him now.

She got to work and spread newspaper out on the floor in front of the television—she didn't want the contaminated files to touch anything in her house. She ran downstairs, double-checked the lock on the alley door, grabbed the box of damp papers and brought them upstairs. She donned thick yellow vinyl gloves from under the kitchen sink. One by one, she pulled the papers out, made a bit more difficult because of the ill-fitting gloves. She had a system where she wrote the client's name on the manila folder and their initials and date in the upper right-hand corner of each piece of paper, in case the two were separated. This was the first time she actually had to utilize her system.

Deep in thought, sorting the papers, she didn't hear Griff come out of the bathroom until a shadow stretched across the papers. She looked up. His wet hair dripped on the collar of his clean T-shirt, turning it a deeper shade of blue. He had a funny expression on his face.

"Making progress?" he asked.

Kneeling, Sarah leaned back on her heels. "The gloves are slowing me down." The tips of the rubbery gloves were an inch too long for her fingers, making it hard to manipulate the papers.

"Don't you have electronic copies of all that?"

"I do transfer my notes to the computer at the end of the day, but I keep the handwritten copies for reference." She plucked another sheet out of the mess, two more papers stuck to it. "These are what I'd call the masters." She tossed the heap back down. "My biggest concern is that my clients' private information might be out there. I'd never want to betray their trust." She shook her head in frustration.

"We saw the video. There's no way the Amish woman carried files out of that alley."

"I still can't imagine Emma Mae had the nerve to do this." *She has a motive.*

"You okay?" He ran a hand over his wet hair.

"I'll feel better once we find Hannah and your niece."

Griff sat down on the edge of the couch cushion and leaned over to study the papers. The smell of her soap and shampoo on this man did something funny to her stomach. "We will."

They locked gazes and Sarah nodded. She couldn't let herself think differently about him. They were working together. *That's all.*

She cleared her throat, needing to change the subject. "I

tossed your clothes into the washer. I put your wallet on the table. I hope you didn't have any wash preferences."

Griff's eyebrow went up. "Nope. Clean is good."

"Then you're in luck." She peeled off the gloves with a snap and stood up. "I feel like this break-in is distracting you from finding your niece. Please don't feel like you owe me anything."

"I'm going to find her." Griff ran his hands up and down the thighs of his jeans. "We're going to find both my niece and your Amish friend." He pushed off the couch and stood next to her.

She couldn't move around him without making things awkward. So, she stood still. *Very still.*

"The only lead I have is that kid, and we're hung up waiting for his dad to get back to me or Caitlin." He exhaled sharply. "It'd be a lot easier if Chester Gilmore carried a cell phone."

"Yeah…"

"Since Chester Gilmore doesn't…we wait. Together."

"Okay." Sarah hated the squeaky quality of her voice.

"Hey…" He placed his index finger under her chin and tipped it up. Warmth radiated outward from where he touched her skin. Thank goodness the light was dim because her face felt beet red. "We're going to find them. I promise."

She covered his hand with hers and pulled it away from her face. "Please don't make promises you can't keep."

"I never do."

She smiled. She had to be open with him. Trust him. "I don't think chasing down Emma Mae for stealing my files and hurting Gramps," she said, pointing to the mess of papers stinking up the apartment, "is going to help us find Hannah or Lexi. Trust me on that."

"Okay. I do trust you. But we should talk to her. She can't go unpunished."

"It can keep. We need to focus all our energy on finding the young women. This mess can wait."

He searched her eyes. "Your decision." He took a step back, apparently sensing, like she had, that the moment had passed.

"Want some yogurt and granola?"

"Sure, but don't tell the other agents at the bureau." A handsome smile quirked half his mouth. "My buddies always razz me for being a number cruncher. I don't need them to add granola cruncher to their repartee."

Sarah washed her hands at the kitchen sink. "I didn't take you for a man who cared what other people think."

Griff locked eyes with her and something deep lurked in their depths. "Only some people."

CHAPTER 14

*T*he next morning Sarah threw on a pair of sweatpants and a T-shirt and braced herself before she opened her bedroom door.

What was I thinking?

Well, she was feeling vulnerable last night when she invited Griff to crash on her couch. And perhaps she just wanted company, with Gramps in the hospital and all. But this morning awkwardness was the prevailing emotion. She wondered how quickly she could shove Griff out the door. She wasn't in the mood for small talk or sharing the small space of the apartment with a man she had only met a few days ago.

Basically, she wasn't a morning person.

Squaring her shoulders, she drew in a deep breath and opened the bedroom door. Relief swept over her when she spotted the empty couch with the blankets and pillow stacked on one end. The washing machine in the closet was running. A small smile played on her lips. *Handsome and thoughtful.*

The water in the shower was on. Heat pulsed through her

veins. She opened the fridge and relished the coolness. She did a quick inventory: eggs, cheese, milk. Bread sat on the counter. She wasn't much of a breakfast person, but she imagined Griff would be hungry. Besides, it gave her something to do other than think about the fact that Griff was in her bathroom. Taking a shower.

Yes, she'd feed him, then get him out of there.

But we still have to work together to find Hannah and his niece.

Shaking her head, she put on the coffee and got busy making scrambled eggs.

She had just pulled out a bowl and whisk when someone started pounding on the alley door. She flicked her gaze to the clock. Too early for any deliveries. The urgent knocking started up again. Maybe someone had news. She rushed downstairs.

"Hold on," she called as she twisted the lock.

"Sarah, open the door."

She froze and glanced over her shoulder toward the stairs leading to her apartment. Griff was still in the shower. She drew in a deep breath and opened the door. Her father stood directly outside the door and her mother stood two steps behind. If that wasn't a metaphor for something, she didn't know what was.

"Hi…" Prickles raced across her scalp. She hadn't called her parents after Gramps landed in the hospital. He had asked her not to. Quite frankly, she didn't want to, either.

Her father planted his palm on the door, forcing it wider. "You are not going to leave us standing in the alley." Strands of gray peppered his once jet-black hair.

Sarah forced a smile. "No, of course not. Come in." She backed up a few feet, but hardly welcomed them warmly. Quite the opposite. Her first instinct was to get rid of them. "Um…you must have heard about Gramps."

"No thanks to you," her father said. "Mrs. Roberts called

your mother. She heard about your grandfather at the diner. You can imagine our surprise."

"Sweetie, why didn't *you* call us?" her mother said, her voice soft and sweet, never one to stir the pot. "Gramps has been in the hospital for days."

"I'm sorry, Mom, it's been crazy around here." Reluctantly she followed them upstairs and into the apartment, the same one her mom had grown up in. Her mother seemed shorter perhaps due to age or years of submission.

As if cued up for maximum effect, Griff took that exact moment to open the bathroom door, a white towel wrapped around his hips. Pools of sweat gathered under Sarah's arms.

Griff met her gaze, then let it drift toward her parents. "Excuse me. Just need to grab my clothes from the dryer."

Sarah jabbed her finger in his direction, hoping he understood the gesture for *get back in the bathroom and please close the door because my parents are here, oh man, this is awkward.* "I'll grab your clothes."

Griff—thankfully—stepped back into the bathroom and pulled the door over to hide his toned abs and mussed wet hair. Sarah drew in another deep breath through her nose and wondered how much more her fried nerves could handle.

"Hold on a second," she said to her parents. She walked across the small space and yanked open the dryer. She removed his clothes. Not bothering to fold them, she carried them in a bundle and shoved them at him through the narrow opening. "Here you go."

Your parents? he mouthed as their eyes met. She nodded her head slightly. His lips curved into a subtle smile.

Is he actually enjoying my discomfort? Sarah glared at him, but couldn't help the soft smile that formed on her lips. She pulled the door closed and spun around and smiled brightly—too brightly—at her parents, who were still standing in the small space that could hardly be called a foyer.

She asked, "Can I get you some coffee?" *In a to-go cup.*

"What's going on here?" her father asked in an all too familiar tone.

She hoped the folded blankets told him what she felt really wasn't any of his business anyway.

"Griff's an FBI agent. He's in town looking for his niece. We think she might be with an Amish girl who has also gone missing."

Her father looked like a pressure cooker about to explode. "You're still at that?" His tone suggested *that* was playing with Barbies or buying pet rocks. "When are you going to learn that getting involved with those people is only going to cause trouble? They don't want anything to do with us."

Those people.

"Don't worry about it," Sarah said, realizing she sounded like a petulant teenager.

"I worry when your grandfather gets attacked because of your work."

"What...? How...?" she sputtered, then decided to drop it. Guilt swelled in her gut. Her father was the master manipulator and instiller of guilt. But in this case, it was deserved. Sarah pressed her lips together and redirected. "Have you been to the hospital yet?"

"We called the hospital this morning and heard he's doing much better. Some memory issues. But they said visiting hours don't start until nine." Her mother wrung her hands.

Not for the first time, Sarah's heart broke for her mom, who'd had to make the choice long ago between her husband and the rest of her family, including her only child. Her husband won every time.

"He's seems to be doing a little better." Sarah tipped her

head toward the small kitchenette. "Sit down. I'll make us something to eat and we can go to the hospital together."

Her mom opened her mouth, the light in her eyes suggesting she was about to say yes. However, her father shook his head and deep lines formed around his pinched lips. "We'll grab something from the diner. You're obviously busy." He turned toward the door.

"Why don't you wait a minute and meet Griff?"

Her mom surprised her by kissing her softly on the cheek. "We'll see you at the hospital."

Tears pricked the back of Sarah's eyes. The familiar smell of her mother's perfume amplified the degree to which she missed her. Emotion clogged the back of her throat and all she could muster was a quick nod of the head.

Sarah closed the door behind her parents and pressed her forehead to the cool wood, listening to their footsteps grow quieter as they descended the stairs. Once the alley door slammed shut, Sarah yanked open the apartment door and jogged down the stairs to make sure the door was secure.

When she climbed the stairs, she found Griff standing in the entryway. Bare feet poked out from his jeans. He ran his hand over his wet hair and lifted an eyebrow. "Your parents in a rush?"

"Apparently." She brushed past him and grabbed a coffee mug from the cabinet and filled it to the rim. *Griff can get his own coffee*. She had to take her anger out on someone, however passive aggressively. "They weren't too happy that I didn't call them to let them know Gramps was in the hospital."

Griff wrapped his strong hands around the back of the kitchen chair and studied her.

Feeling the intensity of his silent interrogation, she said, "I didn't call because I don't get along with my father. Gramps doesn't care for him much, either. I didn't think the negative energy would be any good for him. Besides, Gramps asked me not to."

"I take it your grandfather is your mother's dad."

Sarah nodded. "Gramps doesn't talk about it too much, but he once told me that he didn't mind that my mom moved away from Hunters Ridge. Small-town life isn't for everyone. What he resented is that my father isolated my mom. Even when I was a kid, I wondered why my mom never had any friends.

"Anyway, I moved to Hunters Ridge when I was a teenager to get away from my father. That made Gramps enemy number one because he allowed me to do what my mother couldn't—get out from under Dad's thumb."

Sarah opened and closed three drawers before she found the whisk in the place that it always was. Her pulse thrummed in her brain with her growing anger. She hated that her father had a way of messing with her head. *Still.*

She whisked the eggs harder than she had intended. Why was she blabbing her life story?

"Is that why you help Amish women leave?"

Sarah rubbed her lips together. She'd have to find her lip balm. "One of the reasons." She shot a quick glance at him over her shoulder. "I only help women who come to me. I'm not about encouraging young women to leave the community. But I want to be a resource for those who feel trapped." She pulled the whisk from the bowl and threw it in the sink. A long, stringy bit of egg slimed the side of the sink. "I had an Amish friend I met when I was a teenager. She ended up drowning in the lake."

Her story was punctuated by Griff's soft release of breath.

She looked up from jabbing at the eggs in the nonstick frying pan, then continued, "The community wrote it off as a tragic accident, but I know there was more to it. She wasn't happy and she felt like she'd never be happy." Sarah turned her face away from Griff to hide the tears filling her eyes. She cleared her throat. "After that, I decided I wanted to become a social worker and help people. Often resources aren't available in small towns. I treat anyone who needs therapy, not just the Amish." Sarah stirred the scrambled eggs methodically, not ready to read whatever might be lurking in Griff's eyes. "Yet I'm still unable to help my own mother."

Her mother's life had become so small.

"You're a good person." Griff's deep voice sounded from right behind her.

Sarah turned around slowly. A small space separated them. Their gazes lingered longer than they should have, considering they were working together. *Only* working together.

She scooted past him and yanked open the fridge and stared into it. "That's a nice sentiment, but you hardly know me to make that call."

"I know enough." There was a scratchy, intimate quality to his voice.

She grabbed the orange juice and set it down on the counter. She grabbed two glasses. "Breakfast is ready if you're hungry."

She could feel Griff watching her as she dished out the eggs onto plates. This was all she could handle right now.

CHAPTER 15

*A*fter breakfast, Griff joined Sarah on the living room floor and helped her sort the papers retrieved from the dumpster. He found her a pair of latex gloves that made it easier to handle the papers than with the oversize kitchen gloves.

"Look for the initials in the upper right corner. I didn't always write the full name. Stack the same initials in piles."

"Is this necessary? We already have a strong indication of who did this." He was struggling to understand why Sarah was holding her punches when it came to the young Amish woman.

"I want to make sure I have all of my files. I hate to think of my clients' private information floating out there." She flattened her hand with wide fingers on the pile in front of her. "Don't read them."

"Wouldn't dream of it." He picked up a piece of paper and wondered what that brown smudge was. Maybe scrambled eggs for breakfast wasn't such a good idea. He inhaled slowly through his mouth.

They worked in companionable silence for a short time

before Griff asked, "How long has your father been in law enforcement?"

"Technically, he's former law enforcement. He retired last year. Or so I hear."

"You don't know for sure?" He posed the question gently, curious but not wanting to pry.

"We're not exactly close. I've lived with my grandpa since I was sixteen." Sarah slid off the gloves with a snap and tossed them next to her on the newspaper covering the area rugs. She reached behind her, planted her palms on the couch cushion and pulled herself up from the floor to sit on the edge of the couch. A faraway look clouded her eyes. "When I got old enough to know how he treated my mother, I couldn't stand it anymore. My mother would never leave him. So, I did."

"They didn't put up a fight?" Griff had stopped sorting the papers and rested his elbow on his bent knee.

"I think my father was happy to be rid of me. No one left in the house to talk back to him." She threaded her fingers and twisted them. "I couldn't let him dominate me like he does my mother."

"And this is why you don't care for law enforcement."

Her eyes widened. "Why do you think that?"

"Well, you had a major tell when I told you I was FBI."

A vertical line formed just above her nose. "Really? What..." She shook her head, dismissing whatever question she was about to ask. "I felt like my dad ran his house like his squad room. No one dared question him."

"Not all people in law enforcement are like that."

Their gazes locked and lingered before she looked down and studied the beds of her nails.

Her father really had the ability to do a number on her head, but he knew better than to point it out. Instead he said, "My dad was a cop, too."

"And you became an FBI agent. Runs in the family."

"Much to my mother's disappointment."

Sarah widened her eyes in surprise. "What mother wouldn't be proud of a son like you?"

A smile tugged at the corners of his mouth before a familiar sadness clawed at the back of his throat. "My dad died of cancer when I was eight."

He heard the sharp intake of her breath. He never shared this story, but he felt compelled to open up to Sarah. Her father's unexpected arrival had exposed her emotions to him, not by her choice. He thought maybe sharing himself would even things out. "That left my mom with me and my sister. The rest of the cops were like uncles to me my entire life. Filling in at every father-son activity, helping around the house, and making sure I stayed out of trouble."

"I'm sorry about your dad."

"It was a long time ago."

"You decided to follow your dad into law enforcement. Why FBI?"

"My mom and I came to an agreement. Go to college and get a safe, steady job. I got my CPA license, but I still couldn't settle in. When I learned the FBI needed forensic accountants, it seemed like a no-brainer. My mom capitulated. Crunching numbers behind a desk with the FBI was a solid compromise." Neither he nor his mom ever acknowledged that anyone—regardless of profession—would eventually die, some at a younger age than others. "Losing my dad at such a young age made her overprotective."

"I can imagine." Sarah cleared her throat. "You and your sister must be close."

"We are. My sister's a single mom. I feel like I've let her down. My niece down."

Sarah looked up with a question in her eyes.

"I started moving through the ranks of the FBI and I

didn't have as much time to spend with my nieces as I used to. Lexi got lost in her parents' separation. Acted out."

"You can't blame yourself."

He expected that response from people, but he couldn't accept it. He was Lexi's uncle. He should have been there for her. And her father was a self-involved jerk.

"I bet you're a fantastic uncle." Sarah smiled.

Griff leaned back and rested his elbow on the couch cushion, careful not to touch the fabric with his dirty hands. "I've been thinking about our next step. We've already struck out with Lexi's friends. Why don't we talk to some of Hannah's? See if any of them ever took a ride from Nick Gilmore. He claims he doesn't pick up fares, but I don't believe him."

"What if he's not lying?" Sarah asked, her tone weary.

"I think he is."

Sarah leaned forward and tapped his leg with the side of her fist. "Hannah is friends with Lorianne Graber. She's a little more worldly than most Amish girls." She pulled her hand away and smiled sheepishly. "Why not? Let's talk to Lorianne."

"Any relation to Elmer?"

Sarah nodded. "Sister."

"Interesting. How do you know her?"

"She keeps the books for Cooper and Sons Lumber. Our paths cross because of the hardware store."

"Amish women work outside the home?"

"Well, she did quit to return home, but that didn't last long. She ended up coming back to work. She'll most likely leave once she gets baptized into the Amish faith and marries. She'll stay home and take care of the house. Raise kids. All that wholesome stuff."

"You say it as if that's a bad thing." Griff tilted his head and studied her.

"I don't think it's a bad thing if that's what you want to do." Sarah pushed to her feet and went into the kitchen area and washed her hands.

"Do you think Lorianne might have plans to leave the Amish?"

"I don't." Sarah turned back around slowly, drying her hands with a paper towel. "But I've been wrong before."

Before Griff could question her more, her phone rang.

Sarah frowned and the color drained out of her face when she looked at the display. "It's the hospital."

The small lobby of the country hospital was quiet. A young man in an oversize security uniform that made him look like he was playing dress-up glanced up from his phone. He squared his shoulders and if she hadn't been watching him closely, she might have missed the slight wiggle in his seat, perhaps to make him sit taller. Sarah stifled a grin.

The guard cleared his throat. "May I help you?"

Sarah suspected he was talking an octave lower than he normally did. This time, she failed at hiding a smile. *Don't be in a hurry to grow up, young man.* "Yes, we're here to see Russell Bennett," Sarah said, reaching into her purse to grab her wallet.

The young man clicked a few keys on the keyboard, then looked back up at them. "ID, please."

She slid her driver's license out of her wallet while Griff handed over his FBI credentials.

That made the young man's eyes widen. "Is there something going on in the hospital I should be aware of?" The young security guard's voice cracked.

"No, I'm visiting a friend," Griff said in an even tone. "I'm not here on FBI business."

The security guard's shoulders collapsed, and the hope of a more exciting day drained from his young face. "That's good to know," he lied. He absolutely hoped something exciting was going down at Hunters Ridge Memorial Hospital. The guard scanned both IDs and then handed over two visitor stickers. "Please wear this in a visible location."

"Thanks." Sarah took both stickers, slapping hers on below the shoulder, and she playfully stuck Griff's on his broad chest. She smiled up at him and her cheeks grew fiery. This man had to work out. A lot.

When they reached Gramps's wing, she slowed her pace. Her father's booming voice echoed down the hall. *The reason Gramps had the floor nurse call me.*

Immediately, Sarah's mood soured, and she had an overwhelming urge to duck into an empty room or a linen closet —anywhere to avoid another confrontation. But Griff gave her the strength to keep walking at a brisk pace.

Besides, this was exactly why she had dropped everything and rushed over to the hospital: the nurse said Gramps was agitated, but he wouldn't come right out and ask his visitors to leave.

She cut a quick gaze, trying to read Griff's expression.

He slowed and lifted his hand. "I'll be in the waiting room down the hall."

"Come with me."

Sarah punched the blue square on the wall. The automatic doors to Gramps's floor whooshed open. She found herself holding her breath as her parents came into view.

Her stomach churned. She had expected to find her parents in her grandfather's room, not standing in the hallway. "Hello. How's Gramps doing?"

"Much better." Her mother's voice was soft and pleasing. She was forever trying to fit into a nice, pretty box so as not to offend anyone.

From the time Sarah hit puberty and realized how her mother forced herself to meld perfectly into her husband's life, she vowed never to do the same for *anyone*. Not even her own father. She recognized the undue influence he had over every aspect of her mother's life.

Sarah would never let someone control her like that.

"Let's talk in here." Her father stepped into a small room where Anderson Cooper on a flat screen talked to six empty chairs. They all followed, but none of them sat down.

The need to check on Gramps made her nerves hum. "What's wrong?" She crossed her arms over her chest and glared at her father.

"Russ needs to come to Buffalo." Her father's pronouncement put Sarah further on edge.

"Does he need care that Hunters Ridge Memorial can't provide?" Her gaze drifted from her father to her mother, who immediately lowered her gaze to the gray carpet. Dark spots indicated where gum chewers had missed the trash can, assuming they had even been aiming for it in the first place.

Griff touched her arm softly and leaned in close to her ear. His fresh soap scent tickled her nose. "I'll wait out in the hall," he whispered.

Sarah reached down and squeezed his hand. Thankfully Griff took her cue and stayed by her side.

Her father seemed to regard Griff like a fly that needed to be swatted but wasn't worth the effort because it was harmless even if it was annoying. "I think it's best if Russ moves into a nursing home."

Sarah's stomach dropped. "A nursing home? Is he really that bad? Don't the doctors think he'll improve?" Her voice cracked over the last word and a rush of dread heated her face.

"It's time, Sarah." Her mother's tone was softer and flatter than usual. Sarah could imagine her father saying the exact same thing and her mother was just repeating his words. Forever pleasing her husband.

Who needs that hassle?

"What do you mean, it's time?" Sarah said, her voice growing louder. "Isn't he getting better?"

"It's not that, dear," her mother said, forever trying to appease everyone. "He's old—"

"Hold up." Sarah lifted her hand and anger propelled her closer to her father. "You want to stick him in a nursing home because he's old." She jutted out her chin. "The doctor expects he'll make a full recovery, so I don't see why he can't return to his apartment here."

"Nobody's sticking anyone anywhere." Her father laughed in a condescending tone. "Don't be melodramatic."

Don't be melodramatic. His favorite way to shut down the women in his life.

"Be realistic. He can't do the stairs to the apartment." An annoyed expression flashed across his face. "Besides, business can't be very good." He crossed his arms over his broad chest. "Hunters Ridge is dying." Another slam against his wife who used to love this town until she went to Buffalo for college and met Sarah's father.

Sarah choked back the bile tickling her throat. The longer she was out from her father's house, the harder it was to not lash out at him.

Why are you holding back? Gramps has always been there for you. Speak up.

She took another step toward her father, just shy of getting in his face. "This town is not dying and neither is Gramps. He's staying here with me." She met her mother's concerned gaze. "Mom, you're welcome here anytime. I know Gramps misses you."

"I—"

Her father held up his hand, cutting off his wife. Something akin to glee swept across his face. "Who has been running the store since Russ's been in here?"

Sarah rocked back on her heels.

"That's my fault, sir," Griff said. "My niece is missing and I'm not familiar with Hunters Ridge. Your daughter has been a huge help."

"You've found your niece?" Her father's voice held no emotion.

"Not yet."

Her father turned toward Sarah, his eyes mocking her. "Russ can't run the store alone, and every day you keep the doors locked is another nail in the coffin. People are going to go elsewhere." He lifted a cocky eyebrow, fully enjoying his position of power. "I am not going to spend my pension keeping a dying business alive just so Russ can tinker with projects behind the counter. He can find new projects once he's settled in his new place."

Sarah turned toward her mother, knowing full well her father was a lost cause. "You can't put Gramps in a nursing home."

"Honey, I know it's hard…"

Sarah shook her head. "I'm going to take care of Gramps here in Hunters Ridge." She grabbed Griff's hand and pulled him out of the waiting room.

She dropped his hand once they were in the hall. She strode toward Gramps's room, her heart ready to explode out of her chest. She paused to collect herself before entering, then forced a big smile and stepped into his room.

Gramps had his eyes closed and his skin had a grayish-ashen hue, and she had a flash of her beloved Gramps laid out in an open casket. She shook the image away and approached the bed.

She touched his hand and spoke softly. "Hi, Gramps."

He opened one eye and a slow smile curved his thin mouth. "Hi there." One bushy gray eyebrow twitched. "Is your father gone?"

Sarah couldn't help but return his smile. "He's leaving the hospital now. With mom."

Gramps shook his head. "I didn't raise your mom to be like that."

Sarah covered his hand. "I know, Gramps. Just get better so we can get you out of here."

"Working on it." Gramps adjusted the head of his hospital bed to sit up. "Have you two found the young women you're looking for?"

"Not yet."

"I'm sure you will." Gramps creased the edge of the white blanket covering his thin legs. "Did your father tell you he wants to put me out to pasture?"

"I'm not going to let that happen."

"Maybe it *is* time." Sweet Gramps never wanted to be a burden to her, but he'd never be that. He was there when she felt alone and adrift. He took her in as a teenager.

"Get your strength back, get out of here, and then decide what you want to do. Maybe we can buy a one-story house in Hunters Ridge." Then they could rent out the apartment above the store for extra income. It would be a challenge to fill the space, but not impossible. Threads of hope twined their way through her chest. "But even if we do that, we can still keep the hardware store up and running. We could hire a few people to work the register."

Her grandfather rubbed his bruised head. "We'll figure it out. We always do."

She loved that about her grandfather. Everything and anything was doable—the complete opposite of her controlling father.

CHAPTER 16

*H*annah tugged her long skirt over her legs and hugged them to her chest, trying to keep warm. For the first time in a long time, she was glad plain clothing was modest. The extra fabric allowed her to stay moderately warm, unlike Lexi who was shivering in her short skirt and sleeveless top.

Each day dragged into the next. Hannah had lost track of time and had grown numb. Lexi had gone from tough to falling apart.

Neither had risked eating the food, and Hannah's stomach growled. They only drank water from sealed bottles. *Thank God for that.* They needed to stay lucid for the next time the man paid them a visit.

Hunger was making her weak. And irritable. Lexi had all but stopped talking. She was curled up on the floor of the loft with her back to Hannah. She had gathered what little straw she could to use as a blanket.

"Something is keeping him away," Hannah said, mostly talking out loud because she was tired of the silence. "Maybe something happened to him."

Lexi rolled over and sat up with a mumbled groan. She brushed at the straw. Her long hair was matted on one side with bits of straw poking out. The chain rattled as she straightened her legs. "I hope he's dead." Anger flashed in her eyes.

"If he's dead, no one will find us," Hannah said, tucking her hands under her long sleeves. She wished she could somehow help Lexi get warm. Thankfully the temperatures were mild, but dampness from the rain and their growing frailty had chilled them all the same.

"Next time he comes up here, I'm going to push his sorry butt off the ledge."

"There has to be another way." Hannah couldn't imagine hurting someone.

"I could go for some tacos," Lexi said, changing the subject.

"I've never had tacos. What are they?" Hannah asked, grateful for something to keep her mind occupied, but food probably wasn't the best option.

Lexi plucked a bit of straw out of her hair and flicked it to the ground. "Really?" She seemed to consider it a moment. "It's a tortilla, which is flat bread, with beef and tomatoes and…" She seemed to get lost in the thought for a moment. "Oh, man. We're not going to die up here, are we?" Lexi crawled over to the stacked bales where they had hidden their uneaten food because they didn't want him to know what they had been doing.

"Stop!" Hannah lunged toward her, but Lexi was faster—she moved back toward the far side of the loft, knowing full well that Hannah's shackles limited her range of motion. "Please, don't eat that. There could be poison."

Lexi studied the biscuit.

"Please…" Hannah hated the desperate tone of her voice.

A creaking sound made her heart jump into her throat.

"He's coming," Hannah whispered. "Please…" She felt Lexi's eyes on her, then the girl tossed the biscuit away and quickly moved to the front of the hay bale and sat down.

Hannah let out a slow, long breath and waited.

"The second he gets close to the ledge…" Lexi whispered, her tone desperate.

Each creak of the rungs on the ladder competed with the thundering of her heart. How close was he? The shadows in the old barn were playing tricks on her eyes. She had lost track of time. She leaned forward and squinted, then rocked back on her heels. It wasn't dark outside, but the light was fading.

Finally, a dark shape emerged. A line of light caught the whites of his eyes. He was staring right at Hannah.

A tray of food skidded across the loft floor and he climbed the rest of the way up. Lexi had closed her eyes, but Hannah suspected she was watching him through slits.

"Oh Lexi, rise and shine, dinner's here." The man stepped up onto the loft, oh so close to the edge. Nausea roiled in her gut. Could Lexi really push him off?

Then what?

Hannah swallowed hard and found her voice. "She's been sleeping for a long time." Her tone was even, concerned, but not overly. She could play along. Let the man think they were eating the food that was making them tired.

"Why aren't you sleeping?"

Panic sent goose bumps racing across her skin. "I woke up when I heard you coming."

The man seemed to regard her for a moment, then dismissed her. Amish women were often easily dismissed.

He approached Lexi with curiosity. Perhaps he had poked her, shaken her. Whatever he had done was blocked from Hannah's view. His head swiveled around as if it was on a stick. "You're not asleep," he spat out, each word in an accusatory tone.

Hannah heard jangling, then a snick of a lock. "Are you letting us go?" Her voice squeaked and she immediately regretted it. He leaned close to her and she could smell the sweat off him.

"I'm letting her go." He hoisted Lexi to her feet. Her eyes widened in surprise and met Hannah's. The terrified look on the *Englisch* girl's face sent terror pulsing into Hannah's heart.

"Take me with you. Don't leave me here," Hannah begged.

"You don't want to go where she's going." He pushed Lexi toward the ladder and followed. If she tried anything, she'd be sorry.

Lexi's sobs grew quieter until Hannah was left alone. She bowed her head and cried.

CHAPTER 17

Sarah twisted from side to side on the stool behind the counter in the hardware store. "I feel like I'm being deceitful, asking Lorianne to come here under false pretenses." Sarah had claimed the hardware store had an open invoice from the lumberyard and she wanted to review it before paying it, since Gramps was in the hospital and all.

Griff rested his forearms on the glass counter. "You're doing this to find Hannah. And hopefully Lexi. She'll understand once you have a chance to explain."

Sarah forced herself to stop fidgeting. She hated to think of Griff sitting here when his niece was missing. What if talking to Lorianne was a waste of time?

As if reading her mind, he said, "It's a solid idea. Lorianne and Hannah are friends. And it's likely Lorianne has called Mr. Gilmore for a ride. It can't hurt to hear what she has to say."

An unsettling question flittered around the edges of her brain. If Chester had given Lexi and Hannah rides, where were they now? And where was Chester? Why hadn't he been in touch with them?

Just as the reality of that question made a shudder course through her, the bells on the front door jangled. Sarah pushed off the stool. The sight of sweet, innocent Lorianne strolling in with a basket holding the paperwork made Sarah's cheeks burn.

"Hi, Sarah." Lorianne had a peach complexion and bright, curious eyes.

"Hi, Lorianne." Sarah held her hand up to Griff. "Have you met my friend Griff?"

A thin line creased her forehead. "You're looking for your niece, right? I hope you found her." If Lorianne had been upset that Deputy Flagler came out to their family farm to accuse her brother, Elmer, of attacking her grandfather, there was no hint of it.

"We haven't found her."

"I'm sorry to hear that." The young Amish woman set her basket on the counter and turned to Sarah. "I want to assure you my brother had nothing to do with the break-in here. He's been stuck at home since his poor decision to harass Miss Violet."

Sarah smiled, trying to make her feel welcome. "I know your family has been through a lot." She couldn't imagine what it would be like to lose a sister to murder. "I hope we didn't add to your pain."

"I keep myself busy." Lorianne pulled out a few papers. "How is your grandfather?"

"Getting stronger every day. He'll be back behind the counter in no time."

Lorianne adeptly turned the conversation back to the reason she had been summoned here. "These are the recent invoices from the hardware store."

Sarah and Griff locked gazes, then Sarah turned to Lorianne. "We're not concerned about an invoice."

"Oh?" The Amish woman's face grew pink. "Why…?" She

clumsily gathered up the papers and stuffed them back into the basket.

"We wanted to discuss Hannah. I know you're friends." Sarah studied the woman's face.

Lorianne took a step back, a mask of denial settling in her features. "Friends? We knew each other. I mean, we all do."

Sarah understood why an Amish woman in good standing would want to distance herself from someone who had left the community.

Lorianne dipped her head. "You shouldn't have put me in this position."

"I'm sorry." Sarah really was. "We won't keep you long. I have an important question for you. Have you used Mr. Gilmore's van service?"

"Recently?" The young Amish woman's voice cracked, and her eyes skirted the edges of the hardware store as if she were searching for something specific. Perhaps a way out.

"Any time," Griff jumped in. "Have you called Mr. Gilmore for a ride. *Ever?*"

"Why?" Lorianne lifted the basket and settled the handle on the crook of her arm, as if she was going to turn and leave.

Sarah resisted the urge to touch Lorianne's arm. Something had spooked her, and she didn't want her to run out of the hardware store.

"If you'd like to talk in private, we can go into my office." Sarah coaxed her.

"We can talk here, but I need to sit down."

"Of course." Before Sarah had a chance to move, Griff strode to the office and grabbed a chair. Sarah went to the front door and twisted the lock to assure they wouldn't be interrupted.

"Can I get you something to drink?" Griff asked.

"No, I'm fine." The Amish woman plucked at the folds of

her long skirt. "I have taken Mr. Gilmore's van. He gives rides to lots of the Amish." Her mannerisms and coloring suggested there was far more to this statement, but Sarah didn't want to push.

Griff dragged up a second chair and Sarah sat down and leaned forward, resting her forearms on her thighs. "I don't care if you broke the rules of the *Ordnung*."

Lorianne lifted her eyes and seemed to be weighing her words carefully. "I have called Mr. Gilmore for a ride, but I'd never call him again."

Sarah's pulse beat wildly in her ears.

"A few weeks ago, I was at a Sunday singing." The Amish youth gathered to socialize every other Sunday. "I thought one of the boys I liked was going to take me home in his courting wagon. When he asked Ruth instead, I was mortified." The young woman's cheeks grew pink at the memory. "I was embarrassed and didn't want to ask my friends for a ride." She lifted her eyes slowly, then dropped them to the hardwood floor. "That's what you get for being prideful."

Sarah threaded her fingers and listened patiently. She wanted to reassure the young woman that she had done nothing wrong, but she feared if she spoke, Lorianne might shut down for good.

Lorianne looked up again, uncertainty shining in her eyes.

Sarah smiled softly to reassure her.

"One of my friends has a cell phone. I asked her to borrow it. I never said why."

"One of your Amish friends?"

"*Yah.* We're not supposed to have phones, but we do a lot of stuff we're not supposed to do." She adjusted the strap of her bonnet. "I mean, once we get baptized and married, we don't do that stuff anymore."

"It's okay," Sarah said, trying to stuff down her mounting frustration.

Normally in her practice, she was more patient. But with each hesitant word, Sarah felt the clock ticking down on Lexi and Hannah. Something in her gut told her that time was a luxury they couldn't afford. She still didn't know if their disappearances were related, but she felt like she was perched on the edge of a cliff and the earth was about to give way.

"Who showed up?" Griff peeled away from the wall. While Sarah liked to believe she was quietly impatient, his body vibrated with restlessness.

"Nicky Gilmore."

"His son." Griff slammed his fist down on the counter and the glass vibrated. "I knew that kid was a liar."

Sarah held up her hand to calm Griff. "Something happened, didn't it?" She reached out and covered Lorianne's hand and was surprised when the young woman didn't pull away. "You don't have to tell me, but you might feel better. And it might help us stop him from hurting someone else."

Lorianne shook her bonneted head. "I got away."

"What do you mean?" Sarah could barely hear Griff's question over her pounding heartbeat.

"He refused to take me home. He…" A single tear trailed down her cheek.

Sarah shot a glance at Griff, then focused her attention back on Lorianne. "Talk to me. You're safe here."

Lorianne pulled her hand out from under Sarah's. She clasped her hands and twisted them together. "It was dark, and he tried to take me down a path in the woods." She brushed the back of her fist across her cheek. "I thought maybe he wanted to park, like the youth sometimes do. When I told him to please take me home, he got really angry. He told me I wasn't going home. He called me a tease. Said we were all teases, with our prim and proper clothing. That we were asking for it." Lorianne breathed in and out heavily through her nose. "He took this back road. It was so dark. But then he stopped. He had to get out to move a branch from the road. So I jumped out and ran."

Sarah's heart broke for this young woman. "Did you report the incident?" She already knew the answer.

"I couldn't. My parents had been through so much with my sister's murder...and then my brother." She shrugged. "What if no one believed me? What if they thought I wanted to go to the road alone with an *Englischer*? I've seen girls' reputations ruined for far less. The bishop has warned the youth that they need to get in line. There has been too much turmoil in Hunters Ridge. He said he was going to punish anyone who took their problems to an outsider. He said he has ways of finding out our secrets."

Anger ticked in the back of Sarah's head. The bishop was talking about her. He was scaring them into staying away from her.

"You didn't do anything wrong. I promise," Sarah said. A long-ago memory of her mother sitting on her bedroom floor crying, saying she had nowhere to go, floated to mind. Sarah refused to allow any other woman to feel that way. Not if she could help it. "You have options. I can help you."

"You wouldn't understand..." Lorianne sniffed. "You're an outsider. The bishop will know."

Sarah slumped into the chair. She tried hard to respect the Amish, but the tough love they doled out felt too much like the iron fist her father ruled by.

Lorianne let out a shaky breath. "I don't want to leave Hunters Ridge. I love my family. I can't hurt them." She wiped her tears with both hands, then looked up with wide eyes. "Did the Gilmores' son hurt someone?"

"My niece's phone was found at the Gilmores' house," Griff said.

Lorianne nodded, suddenly growing confident. "Something is wrong with the son. The devil has gotten a hold of his heart."

Griff crouched down to be at eye level with Lorianne. "Do you think you could show us the road he took you down? Then I promise we'll take you back to the hardware store or wherever you want to go."

"Mr. Cooper gave me a ride into town. He told me to call him when I was ready to go home. I'm done with my work at the lumberyard for the day."

"Call him. Tell him you found another ride. *Please.* We need your help. We have no intention of getting you into trouble with the bishop." Sarah stood and smiled softly at Lorianne. She couldn't help but think how conflicted some of these young women must feel. "Can you help us?"

"Yes." Lorianne squared her shoulders and stood with the confidence of a woman who knew she had to help her friend, no matter what the consequences. "I can show you."

CHAPTER 18

"*T*urn here!" Lorianne pointed toward a narrow opening between the trees, just wide enough for a car to slip through. No one would know it was there unless they were looking for it.

Griff slowed, and turned his truck onto the path. His tires sunk into the soft earth. He cut a quick glance at Sarah who sat silently in the passenger seat.

"How far did you go along this path?" he asked.

"Not far. A tree had fallen, so he had to get out to move it." Lorianne leaned through the opening between the seats to get a better view out the windshield. "About here. He got out and I waited until he was struggling with the branch and I jumped out and ran through the woods. *Gott* was watching over me. That guy was up to no good."

"Did he chase you?"

"I don't know. I never stopped running. I cut through the fields until I got home." Lorianne sounded breathless as she finished her story.

"It wasn't your fault," Sarah said.

Griff wondered how she was able to work with young

women who had such different backgrounds. How did you convince an Amish woman that she had not brought evil upon herself because she got in a van with a creepy guy?

Lorianne seemed to be studying the dark shadows under the trees where she had made her escape. "Aren't you going to turn around?" Her voice grew shaky. "I only went as far as there."

"It's okay," Sarah said. "We need to go farther. See where Nicky was heading before he got out of the car."

"But it's getting late. My family will wonder where I am. I already missed helping my *mem* with dinner." Lorianne slid back and sat stiffly against the seat.

Griff watched her in the rearview mirror. Her wide eyes darted from window to window searching the landscape. "We'll make sure you get home," Griff said. "I have to see where this leads."

Griff's truck bobbled over the ruts. In a few places his tires spun in the mud before gaining traction. Deep tracks showed him the way. "Someone's been down here recently."

"Yeah…" Sarah tugged on her seat belt.

"Maybe you can take me home first," Lorianne said. "I'll get in trouble."

"A little farther." He was afraid if someone was out here and saw his tire tracks, he wouldn't get a second chance to make a surprise visit.

A canopy of trees opened to a field. A run-down barn sat in the opening. About a football field away, a house with a hole in the roof had seen better times. "Do you know if anyone lives here?" he asked.

"*Neh.*"

"It looks abandoned," Sarah said.

"But someone has been here recently." His heart raced in his chest. All the pieces were lining up. Nicky had tried to take Lorianne down this lane, and Griff suspected she had escaped something far worse than a ruined reputation.

Griff slammed the gear into Park. "Stay here."

Sarah looked like she wanted to protest, but then thought better of it. Someone had to stay with Lorianne. He reached across Sarah's lap and grabbed his gun out of the glove box.

He gave a quick nod to Sarah as he climbed out of the truck. "Lock the doors. I'll be right back."

He closed the door quietly, hoping to maintain the element of surprise. The mud sucked in his shoes as he crossed the field. The early evening was completely silent, as if all the insects and critters knew the enormity of the situation. He reached the barn and walked the perimeter. He found an opening on the far side. Pressing his back against the wall to minimize the risk of being a target, he peered into the opening. *Gray shadows.*

He struggled to listen over the raggedness of his breath, his nerves rioting. Was he truly this out of practice in the field? Or were the personal stakes sending him into hyperdrive?

Griff slid into the barn, then ducked back into the shadows. An overpowering scent of damp hay and rotting fruit reached his nose. He strained to listen. For someone breathing. For someone ready to attack.

A rattling of a chain sounded from somewhere up and to his left.

"FBI," he shouted. "I'm armed."

The rattling grew louder and more frantic. "Up here! I'm up here!"

"Are you alone?" he hollered, glancing around, his eyes adjusting to the shadows.

"*Yah.* Help, I'm chained up."

Griff holstered his gun and then pulled out his cell phone. He swiped on the flashlight app and pointed it in the direction of the woman's voice. He did a quick scan of the interior of the barn to make sure a surprise wasn't lurking in the shadows. "Are you in the loft?"

"*Yah*, hurry before he comes back."

Griff shone the beam of light around the barn until he found a ladder lying on its side. He propped it against the edge of the loft. He tested his weight on the bottom rung before he began his ascent. When he reached the top, he found a woman, her eyes wide, her knees pressed to her chest. She wore a bonnet and long dress.

"Hannah Shetler?"

She nodded and then rested her forehead on her knees and broke down in tears.

Griff crossed the small space. "Are you okay?"

Hannah nodded. Her lower lip trembled. "He has me chained to the wall."

"Who did this to you?"

"Nick Gilmore."

A shudder coursed down Griff's spine at the mention of the name of the man who had been their suspect all along. He flashed the beam of the flashlight around the space, careful not to direct it into Hannah's eyes. A second chain was affixed to the wall. A metal bracelet hung from the end. "Has he held anyone else here?"

"*Yah*. An *Englisch* girl."

"Do you know her name?" Griff's pulse whooshed through his veins like molasses as he held his breath, waiting for her reply.

"*Yah*." She drew in a shaky breath. "Lexi. I don't know her last name."

Dots danced in his eyes. The urge to vomit was strong. His sweet niece had been shackled to this wall. "Where is she?" His mind raced. *Calm down.* He couldn't lose it now.

Hannah pressed her lips together and shook her head. "I don't know. He came and took her away."

"When?"

"Earlier today."

"What did he say?"

Hannah kept shaking her head. Griff drew in a deep breath and focused on the moment. He glanced at the screen on his cell phone and prayed for a few bars. They appeared.

Thank goodness for small favors.

"I'll get you out of here. I'm going to call the sheriff's department." Griff detailed his location to the dispatcher. "I have to go; I'll be right back." He had to let Sarah and Lorianne know that their friend was safe.

Hannah reached out and grabbed his wrist. A frantic look sparked in her eyes. "Please, don't leave me alone."

"Okay, okay." Griff sat on the edge of a hay bale and dialed Sarah's number.

She must have been holding the phone in her hand because she answered immediately.

"I found Hannah."

Sarah lifted her head and said a silent prayer of gratitude before she overthought it. She wrapped her hand around the car door handle, ready to run out and meet them in the barn. She held the phone out in front of her on speaker mode.

"Stay in the truck. Make sure the doors are locked." Griff's solid voice filled the vehicle.

A quiet yet terrified squeak came from the back seat. Sarah considered taking the phone off speaker, but Lorianne deserved to know what was going on. She had led them here. Without her, they would have never found Hannah.

Sarah searched her surroundings, her heart thrumming in

her chest. The thick foliage on the trees created plenty of shadows to hide in.

"Is he here?" Lorianne asked, staring into the trees.

"There's no sign of him," Griff said, "but I can't take any chances."

"Can't you come out?" She hated the neediness of her question, but she felt exposed. Anyone could be watching her from the protection of the woods.

"She doesn't want me to leave her alone. I've called Deputy Flagler. Stay in the truck until you see a patrol car, okay?"

"Of course."

Lorianne had slid forward and was leaning on the console. Hope brightened her eyes. "Is Hannah okay?"

"She will be," Griff said, his answer curt.

"What about Lexi?" A flush of dread warmed every inch of her skin at the thought of what these young women might have been through.

A long pause filled the space, so long she thought they might have been disconnected.

"Griff?" She held the phone farther away and glanced down at it. The green edges still glowed.

"Lexi's not here." The flatness of his tone sent a chill up her spine.

"Oh no…" A solid band squeezed her lungs, making it difficult to breathe. "We were wrong. They weren't together." Guilt swept over her. She had distracted him from finding his niece. "I'm so, so sorry."

"We weren't wrong." Griff sounded strangely calm. "Lexi was here. The kid came and got her a few hours ago." The words *a few hours ago* hung heavy in the air.

"Does Hannah know where he took her?" Sarah's voice cracked and she sucked in a breath, waiting for him to answer.

"No." His curt answer made her heart break.

A flashing red and blue light cut across the thick foliage. "A patrol car is here."

"Okay, good. Tell Caitlin that we're in the loft. Tell her to bring bolt cutters."

"Okay. Okay." Sarah struggled to process this. *Bolt cutters?* "I'll tell her."

Sarah ended the call and opened the truck door. A cloud of insects swarmed her sweaty head. When she turned around to slam the door, the window reflected dark shadows under her eyes.

They had found Hannah, but where was Lexi?

CHAPTER 19

*G*riff needed a moment.

He sat on the edge of his bumper in the middle of the clearing near the abandoned barn where Lexi had been held only hours ago. He jammed his hands through his hair.

Where is she? His sweet watch-me-ride-my-bike niece? The little girl he had loved like his own, especially since her father was a first-rate jerk. His stomach churned. Oh, he'd have to call his sister. This was his worst nightmare realized.

A gentle hand rested on his shoulder. He knew it was Sarah, but he couldn't meet her eyes. They'd be filled with sympathy and affection, neither of which he deserved. He had failed his niece.

"Everything's going to be okay."

"No, it's not." He stepped away from her touch. "I should have gotten here sooner."

"You—"

"Stop, I don't need you feeling sorry for me. It's Lexi we need to worry about." He pressed the heels of his hands into his eyes, then dropped them. He was being a complete jerk to Sarah, but he couldn't help himself. He rolled his shoulders and exhaled sharply, trying to settle his nerves. The arrival of the two sheriff's patrol cars had lit up the scene like a movie set in the middle of the night.

Ugh, if only this was a movie. Or a nightmare I could wake up from.

Tears welled in his eyes.

He blinked slowly, then shook his head. No, he'd had his moment. Now he was back in FBI mode. He crossed over to Caitlin. "Are Hannah and Lorianne all set?" he asked.

"Yes, the ambulance took Hannah to the hospital. She claims he poisoned them and kept them locked up. But other than that, she says he didn't do anything...but she might be afraid to talk to us."

Griff nodded. *Stay focused.* "And Lorianne?"

"I had one of the other deputies take her home."

"Okay, we have to get a search warrant for the Gilmore house. We have to get in there."

The deputy placed her hand on his forearm. Why did everyone feel the need to touch him? He just wanted to do his job and find his niece.

"Maybe you need to sit this one out."

There it was.

Griff gritted his teeth. "No, I'm not sitting this one out. Either work with me or around me. I'm going to find my niece even if it means breaking a window and punching out this kid's teeth."

Caitlin stared at him for a long minute. "We'll work with you, but you have to promise me you'll let the justice system work. We have to get this guy the right way. We don't want him to get off on a technicality."

"This kid has been working the system already," Griff said, reflecting on the deputy's stories about how Nicky's father and the sheriff were buddies, which meant Nicky never had to deal with the consequences of his actions.

"Hey, that's not fair," Caitlin said. "You know how it is with the chain of command. My hands were tied. Mr. Gilmore is not going to be able to use his connections with the sheriff to get off the hook. Not this time."

Griff closed his eyes briefly and drew in a long breath, trying to rein in his emotions, but he was running out of patience. Lexi was in imminent danger.

"You good?" Caitlin asked.

Griff nodded. "Let's go. I'll take my truck and meet you there. The quieter we do this, the less likely we have a hostage-standoff situation."

"Agreed. But wait for me. The sheriff's department gets first crack at getting into the Potter Road house."

∼

If Caitlin was as good of a deputy as she was a driver, Hunters Ridge was in very good hands. The deputy didn't let off the gas until her patrol car was sitting in the Gilmores' driveway.

Griff pulled up behind her in his truck. Sarah sat quietly in the passenger seat; tension rolled off her in waves. Another patrol car pulled up a minute later. They had made the decision to come in without lights and sirens, but the Gilmore kid and his father would know they were there the second Caitlin's V-8 engine roared up the driveway.

"You okay?" Sarah asked for the first time since he climbed behind the steering wheel. They had both been holding their breaths as they drove over here.

"I'll be better when I find my niece." He refused to call his sister to tell her he had failed again.

"She's here and she's safe."

"From your lips to God's ears." Griff scrubbed a hand across his face. "Let's do this." He pulled on the door handle and the dome light popped on. Evening had gathered quickly. At the last minute, he glanced over his shoulder. "Stay close to the vehicle. We have no idea what this kid is capable of."

Sarah nodded.

Caitlin made her way over to him. Her hand hovered near the butt of her gun in its unclasped holster. "I'll approach the front. The other deputy will go around back in case he tries to bolt. You come with me. Best situation, his father's inside and talks some sense into his son before things go south."

It was Griff's turn to nod. For a guy who spent his FBI career as a forensic accounting analyst, he had seen more action in the past few days than in his whole career. Perhaps he was prone to exaggeration. If his niece wasn't involved, he might admit he loved being in the field.

Caitlin led the way. She lifted her fist and pounded on the door. "Sheriff's department. Open up."

Griff strained to detect any noise—television, footsteps… a scream—coming from inside, but it was quiet. The deputy pounded again. "Open up or we're coming in."

Since Hannah had already pointed the finger at Nicky for kidnapping her and Lexi, they had no reason to wait for a warrant. They had every reason to believe Lexi was in imminent danger.

Caitlin looked up at him, giving him the go-ahead. Adrenaline spiked as he backed up to kick the door in.

Just then, it swung open. Griff had to do everything under his power not to unleash his door-busting skills on this scrawny jerk's gut, bending him in half. At this exact moment nothing would have given him more pleasure.

Except finding Lexi unharmed.

"Sheriff's department. Turn around and put your hands behind your back," the deputy commanded.

Nick blocked the door. His hair was uncombed, and lines creased his face, as if he had been woken out of a deep slumber. "What's going on?" he mumbled.

Without giving him an answer, Caitlin spun him around, handcuffed him and shoved him to a seated position on the front porch.

"Is anyone else home?" Griff asked, his eyes canvassing the area.

Nicky hesitated a moment.

"Is anyone else home?" Griff repeated.

"No. I'm home alone." Nicky finally found his voice.

Caitlin pointed at Nick as another deputy approached. "Keep an eye on him. We're going in."

"You have no right." Nick apparently got a second wind, affording him the energy to be indignant. "I want a lawyer."

"You'll get a lawyer, so why don't you just shut up in the meantime," the deputy said.

Griff really liked this Deputy Caitlin Flagler.

He followed her into the house and the two of them split up to search the premises.

His heart sank when he realized Lexi wasn't here. He wasn't sure what he expected: Lexi sitting in front of the TV watching Netflix? Lexi having a sandwich at the kitchen table? Lexi bound and gagged and tied to the plumbing under the sink in the bathroom?

Anything other than this stillness.

Griff did a double take at the TV room. Something felt different to him from when he was here a few days ago picking up Lexi's phone, but he couldn't put his finger on it. Subtle. But something.

Caitlin stomped down the stairs, holstering her weapon.

"No one upstairs. But there is an external lock on one of the bedrooms. Looks like someone was sleeping there recently."

Griff jammed his hand through his hair. *Where is Lexi?* His gaze drifted to the door.

If Nick refused to tell him where his niece was, he'd make him.

CHAPTER 20

*S*arah leaned against Griff's truck and wrapped her arms around her middle. The porch light illuminated Nicky sitting on the porch with his knees up toward his chest and his hands handcuffed behind his back. She stared at the front door willing Griff to appear with his niece.

Please, God. Please. Her mother, and then her grandfather had taught her to pray daily, not just when she needed something. Praying at all, of late, made her feel like a hypocrite. She figured God would forgive her. Welcome back the prodigal daughter and all that. She quieted her mind and said a heartfelt prayer for Lexi's safe return.

A gust of wind rustled through the leaves. A chill skittered down her spine. She should have felt secure. Safe now that Nicky had been arrested and two patrol cars sat in the driveway. But there were too many unanswered questions.

A faint creak sounded off to her right, drawing her attention.

A quiet clack followed.

Sarah double-checked that Nicky was secure on the

porch under the guard of some fresh-faced deputy. She peeled off the truck where she had been leaning and walked slowly toward the sound.

The old garage stood apart from the rest of the yard. An old-fashioned garage door was open a sliver, the wind making it creak and thud against the frame.

Thud. Thud. Thud.

Heart beating in her hears, Sarah took another step closer to investigate. She reached out and grabbed the door and pulled it open. The white van sat inside the garage.

Strange. Where is Mr. Gilmore? The wind had carried Nicky's response to the deputy that his father wasn't home. Was he out with friends again?

She glanced over her shoulder to see Griff standing with the kid. Her stomach pitched. There was no sign of Lexi.

Sarah leaned close to the van and saw a red smudge on the bumper. Her vision went out of focus for a moment and terror raced through her.

"Griff," she hollered. "You need to see this."

Griff's head snapped up and he ran across the lawn. Hope and expectation lit his features. "What is—" Before he had a chance to finish his question, his eyes were drawn to the van.

The blood.

Griff peeled back the second garage door. "What the…?" He met Sarah's gaze. "This is his father's van, right? Nick just told me his father was running errands. In the van."

Dread swirled in Sarah's gut.

Griff ran back up to the house. He slowed to talk to the deputy and Nick before returning a few moments later with the keys. Slipping on latex gloves, he got behind the wheel and backed it out of the garage. Its headlights illuminated the interior of the garage. Sarah approached the driver's side window and followed Griff's gaze. Any hope had been extinguished from his eyes.

Sarah felt sick.

Griff jumped out of the van and ran into the garage. He scooped tilled earth with his bare hands from what looked like a fresh grave.

~

Griff had never had an out of body experience. Until now.

The sight of the grave would have sent him over the edge if he didn't set himself apart. He was vaguely aware of Sarah hollering to the deputy, of his bare hands digging into the cold dirt, of his prayers begging God to spare his niece.

He wasn't sure how long he had been there when a deputy forcefully took his bicep and drew him to his feet, away from the grave. "I'll do that, sir," the young deputy said. The same one who had been standing guard by Nick.

So where is Nick now?

Griff stepped aside, almost in a trance, and watched as the deputy stabbed dirt with a shovel.

"Be careful." *What if she's buried alive?*

The tool made short work of the grisly task.

He sensed, rather than saw, Sarah's concerned gaze on him.

The deputy kept shoveling until he reached a black tarp.

Griff fisted and unfisted his hands. The deputy planted the sharp edge of the shovel into the fresh pile of dirt he had removed from the grave.

"The M.E. is on her way." Griff spun around to find Caitlin standing behind him. "Nick Gilmore is secure in the back of the patrol car."

Griff's thoughts ran to the macabre as the four of them stared at the tarp. Would the M.E. pull it back to find Lexi's lifeless eyes, waxy skin, and blue lips?

He focused on his breathing. Counting each breath. He was about to jump out of his skin.

"How much longer?" Griff asked, impatient.

The deputy talked into her shoulder radio. "She just pulled up."

Griff nodded.

The medical examiner's presence sucked out what little air was left in the garage. She set her toolkit on the ground near the grave. Without looking at them, she said, "You're going to have to step outside."

Griff shook his head. "It's my niece."

"I'm sorry, sir. But I need you to step outside. I can't work if I think you're going to pass out on my crime scene."

The medical examiner's no-nonsense talk snapped him out of his fog. "Okay, I'm going to be right outside. I need to know if that's my niece that scumbag buried here." Griff was surprised by his even tone when inside a rage stormed so fiercely that he feared he'd tear Nick's head off either way.

Griff stepped out into the driveway. Someone had placed a cracked white plastic chair on the gravel. "Sit down." He tuned into Sarah's voice. "Please."

Caitlin had taken up a watchful pose outside the open garage doors, forcing Griff to comply with Sarah.

He wrapped his fingers around the edge of his seat. "That can't be Lexi in there. It just can't."

Griff searched Sarah's face for confirmation. Or a denial. *Anything.* The wait was excruciating. A single tear tracked down her cheek and twisted his gut. She was going to be his undoing.

Sarah moved behind him and slid her hands down onto his chest. He reached up and held tightly to one of her hands. He needed an anchor to keep from drifting so far out that he'd never return.

He tracked the movement in front of the house. The

deputy who had unearthed the body climbed behind the wheel of his patrol car with the kid in back. As the patrol car bobbled over the ruts, Nick turned to face him through the back passenger window. A slow smile crept up his mug, adding fuel to the fire burning in Griff's gut.

Sarah squeezed his hand, drawing him back from the dark brink. He closed his eyes and tried to calm himself.

The M.E. emerged from the garage. Her hair was pulled tight into a ponytail and clear safety goggles protected her eyes. She wiped something invisible from her cheek with the back of her latex glove.

Griff jumped to his feet and held his breath. Sarah slid her hand around the crook of his elbow.

The M.E. gave him a strained smile. "It's not her."

Griff bowed his head and relief sagged his body. Then his head snapped up. "Are you sure?"

"One hundred percent. It's a male. Approximately age fifty."

Griff narrowed his gaze, waiting for her to say what he now expected.

"It's Chester Gilmore."

"Nicky's father…" Sarah let the words trail off.

The M.E. nodded. "Hazards of working and living in a small town. I tend to know everyone."

"Cause of death?" Griff's mind raced.

"Well, I'll have to do a more thorough autopsy in the lab, but I suspect the large divot in the side of his skull had something to do with his current state." She turned on her heel. "I have to get back in there, but you needed to know that it's not your niece."

"Thank you." His momentary relief that his niece wasn't in the grave was replaced by the familiar nagging question that had been dogging him since his sister called: *Where is she?*

The question was all the more alarming because the man

who had seen her last had killed his father and buried him in the garage.

None of this boded well for his niece.

Caitlin was the last to exit the house. She shook her head. "I'm sorry. There's no sign of your niece."

Griff dragged a hand through his hair. The knot in his chest tightened. "Mind if I walk through one last time?"

The deputy hesitated a minute, then held out her hand in a *go for it* gesture. And she strode away, as if giving permission without actually giving it.

Sarah placed her hand on the small of his back. "We'll find her."

He glanced down at her and frowned. "Something was different about the house. I can't put my finger on it."

Griff held the door for Sarah. The place had been aired out a bit from all the people coming and going, and it no longer smelled of dirty laundry and day-old food. Somewhere in the distance a dog barked. "Upstairs or downstairs?" Sarah asked.

Griff turned toward the TV room. "Here. Something is different." His eye was drawn down. "This rug. It's moved. Not much." He walked around to one end of the couch and lifted it.

Sarah grabbed the other side.

Together they lifted the couch off the rug. Griff bent down and rolled it up. Underneath was the original hardwood floor, discolored in places from the sun, from water, from age. Griff stomped every few inches, trying to determine if it was hollow. That's when he saw it. A small hole. He dropped to his knees and hooked his index finger in it. He made brief eye contact with Sarah before pulling up the trap door. It opened on an invisible hinge.

Underneath the house was a crawl space. He felt Sarah watching him as he trained the beam of light from his cell phone flashlight on the hidden location. He braced himself against the edge of the opening and stuck his head in to look around. When the light swept over a dark corner, he saw Lexi, her head tipped to the side, her eyes closed, and a piece of silver duct tape slashed over her mouth.

His heart dropped. "She's down there." Griff swung his legs around and jumped into the pit. Through the thundering in his ears, he could hear Sarah hollering to the deputies outside to call for an ambulance.

He'd found his sweet, beautiful niece.

"Hey, Lexi, Lexi…" His back scraped across the underside of the house as he moved closer.

He dropped his cell phone on the hard-packed earth, leaving it in flashlight mode. The light hit the rough underside of the house and splashed back. Lexi's face had an otherworldly glow.

"Honey…" Lexi didn't stir.

He reached for her neck and felt a steady pulse. *Thank you, God.*

Gently, he peeled back the duct tape from her mouth. He felt around the back of her to find her hands tied behind a support beam. He undid the knots by feel. He took her into his arms and scooted back to the opening where he was met by Sarah and Caitlin who helped him lift his sweet, sweet niece out of what could have been her grave.

"An ambulance is on the way," Sarah said as she swept Lexi's hair out of her eyes. She smiled at Griff. "You found her."

Griff nodded, but any words got stuck in the emotion clogging his throat.

CHAPTER 21

$\mathcal{T}$he repeated buzzing of a cell phone rustled Sarah out of a sound sleep. She blinked a few times. She had fallen asleep on her bed, fully dressed. She hadn't slept this soundly since she ran into Annie at the grocery store, and now she was going to give this robocaller a piece of her mind. She swept up the phone and answered it without looking.

"I'm on the Do Not Call list, buddy!" she snapped into the phone.

"Um…"

Sarah pulled the phone away from her ear, then put it back up.

"I didn't think *I* was on that list?"

Sarah swung her legs around and sat up on the edge of the bed. *Griff.* She looked at the clock on her bedside table. It was after one a.m. "Is Lexi okay?"

"Her mom's staying with her at the hospital. Early reports say she's going to be fine. Physically, anyway."

"I'm so sorry she had to go through all this." She wiped a hand across her face and dug her toes into the carpet. Her foggy brain was still trying to process why he had to call her in the middle of the night, not that she minded hearing his voice.

"Sarah…"

"Yeah?"

"I'm downstairs."

"Hold on." She ended the call, ran to the mirror, swiped a finger under her eyes, and ran down the stairs and opened the door to the back alley. "Hello."

"Hi." Half his handsome mouth crooked into a grin. He reached out and smoothed a strand of her hair.

Her face grew warm, and she took a step back. "I can put on coffee."

He climbed the steps behind her. She put on the coffee and the two of them settled on the couch. She tucked her knee under her and faced him. "When are you going home?"

"Today." Griff pressed his lips together and nodded.

Sarah struggled for something else to say. Had he come by to say goodbye in person?

Sarah traced the seam on the arm of the couch. "Has Lexi told you what happened?"

"I had a chance to talk to both Lexi and Hannah. Deputy Flagler was with me. Hannah had called for a ride from Mr. Gilmore. The son showed up instead. He told her his father had a job for her if she wasn't ready to go back to the farm. She took him up on it. At first, nothing seemed out of the ordinary. She and another Amish girl shared chores around the house. But soon Hannah got restless and wanted to leave. When she tried to escape, he shackled her in the abandoned barn."

Sarah had so many questions, but Griff seemed to anticipate them.

"Lexi had also called Gilmore for a ride. She said she couldn't get an Uber, so one of the locals told her about this guy who drove the Amish around. Again, Nick showed up instead of his dad. With my niece, he didn't make any pretenses. He took her straight to the barn where he already had Hannah. God knows what his plans were."

"I'm so thankful she's alive. Did she say how her wallet ended up in the abandoned building next to the hardware store?"

"Nick probably tossed it there to throw us off. He mentioned kids hung out at that place." Griff shook his head. "For a dumb kid, he made some smart moves to throw us off the track."

"What about the other girl who was living at the Gilmores' house before Hannah arrived?" Sarah bit her lower lip, praying for good news.

Griff shook his head. "They're trying to track her down. Hannah's sharing what little she knows about her. They searched the entire property with K-9s. She's not there."

"That's awful. I hope she's okay." Sarah bit back her anger. "This is why I help young women. Without help, they tend to be more vulnerable to predators."

"I've contacted my office. We'll find her."

"I hope so." Sarah shook her head slowly. "Why do you think Nicky killed his father?" *Poor Mr. Gilmore.* He had tried to get his son help after he showed violet tendencies toward animals, but like a lot of parents, he figured he'd grow out of it. Or it was a phase. That kids would be kids. Perhaps stopping therapy had been a fatal mistake. Maybe Sarah could have helped him. Maybe not. That was the saddest part of it all.

"Caitlin thinks Mr. Gilmore and his son got into a fight—maybe the elder Gilmore figured out his son was up to something when he returned home from his sister's." Griff shook his head. "He brought Lexi back to the house to clean up the mess. He then dragged Chester's body out to the garage." He continued to shake his head. "I hate to think what would have happened to Lexi if we didn't show up when we did."

"Thank God," Sarah said, placing her palms together.

"I'm sure the local sheriff's department will put all the pieces together. I've got my niece. She's going to have to do a lot of healing, but she's safe."

"And Hannah…" Sarah said.

"And Hannah." Griff pushed to the edge of the couch but didn't stand. "I left the hospital and I wanted to update you in person."

"…in the middle of the night." She let a playful quality fill her voice.

He shifted to face her. "In the middle of the night." His deep voice rumbled over her.

"I didn't get you that coffee." She scooted forward on the couch. The rich aroma of the brewed coffee floated in the air.

He placed his hand on her knee. "I didn't come here for coffee."

Sarah stilled and found herself leaning toward him. He threaded his fingers through her hair and tingles vibrated through her entire body. Half his mouth crooked into a grin, then he closed the distance. His warm lips covered hers. She bit back a groan as the kiss deepened. Placing a hand on his solid chest, she gently pressed away and met his heated gaze. "I'm sorry for the reason we met, but I'm glad we did." She cleared her throat. "I'll miss you."

He tucked a strand of her hair behind her ear, the warmth of his touch trailing across her cheek. "About that…"

She tipped her head. Prickles of awareness coursed across her skin as she waited for him to finish that thought.

"How would you feel about me sticking around?"

She furrowed her brow. "Sticking around?"

Half his mouth quirked into that grin again. She

suspected he knew what it did to her. "Caitlin said they're hiring at the sheriff's department."

A ticking started in her head. "A forensic accountant?"

Griff shook his head. "A deputy. I have to start living my life *for me*. I've always wanted to follow my father's footsteps, but I played it safe to make my mom happy." He shrugged. "I see Hannah and women like her who take big risks in their lives to live the way they want to live. I can no longer let others dictate how I live my life."

Sarah narrowed her gaze. "You realize you're putting me in a bad position."

"Oh yeah?" He arched an eyebrow. A mix of confusion and lightheartedness danced in his eyes.

"Your mom's going to blame *me* for you taking a risky job."

Her face immediately flushed—they had only known each other for less than a week. She was being a bit presumptuous assuming she had anything to do with the reason he was sticking around Hunters Ridge.

She stiffened her back and quickly added, "I guess it's not like you're sticking around on my account."

A slow smile pulled up the corner of his mouth. "You're one of the perks of the new job."

Sarah felt herself mirroring his smile. "Please be safe. I can't handle any more drama in my life."

Griff made a *pfft* noise with his lips before tilting his head and leaning in for another kiss. He pulled back a fraction and whispered, "How much can actually go on in sleepy Hunters Ridge, anyway?"

EPILOGUE

 *ight months later*

Sarah knocked on the door and called out to Gramps. "Are you getting settled?"

Gramps sat on the couch with a box of his belongings next to him. One by one, he pulled items out and set them on the end table. "Almost done." He looked up and smiled. "I don't know what I'll do with all this space."

"You can have a dance party," Sarah joked.

Gramps arched an eyebrow. "I think my dancing days are over." He paused with a wood photo frame in hand. "Are you sure this is no trouble? I don't want to be in the way."

"How could you possibly be in the way?" Sarah patted him on the shoulder as she breezed past and set his favorite coffee grounds on the kitchenette counter, then joined him on the couch, the box between them.

Gramps reached out and took her left hand and studied the diamond ring and band. "He's a good man."

"Yes, he is." Sarah had never thought she'd find a man worthy of a risk. She and Griff had gotten married on Valentine's Day and had bought a house in Hunters Ridge. The renovations were extensive because it had previously belonged to an Amish family. But her favorite part of the property was that it had a *dawdy haus*, as they called it. A perfect detached home for Gramps.

Sarah grabbed another frame from the box. The old photo was of Gramps and her mother at the hardware store. Her mother was clutching a doll.

"I talked to Mom. She said she'd visit."

"We'll see." The estrangement between Gramps and her mom broke her heart.

"And," she said, interjecting a cheery tone, "I'll make sure you get to the hardware store as often as you'd like."

Sarah was still taking clients in the back office, so she'd be going in anyway. But now Gramps didn't *have* to cover all the shifts. Emma Mae, in an effort to make amends for stealing Sarah's files and injuring Gramps in the process, had arranged for a continuous cycle of Amish to work at the store. She had simply claimed that Russ Bennett was a *gut* friend. Gramps and Sarah had kept all of her secrets. Sure, the workers were getting paid, but they were the most reliable and knowledgeable employees Gramps could hope for. Business had been booming because Emma Mae and Timothy had a lot of newlywed friends who were setting up homes of their own. They made a point of shopping at the hardware store instead of the supercenter a few miles down the road. Now Gramps could finally retire. Sort of.

And for her efforts, Emma Mae's secret remained intact. She married Hannah's brother and had their child seven months later. If anyone had been doing the math, they didn't say anything. Perhaps something could be said for only allowing the Amish to have an eighth-grade education. Or perhaps her grandfather, the bishop, was willing to overlook their impropriety for the sake of appearances.

Hannah had also seemed to find her path. She was teaching at the Amish schoolhouse and rumor suggested she was being courted by a nice Amish man. After her terrifying experience, she found comfort in the familiar.

A knock sounded at the door and Griff poked his head in. "Everyone okay here?"

Sarah's heart leapt with joy every time she saw her husband. *My husband.* Never in a million years did she think she'd get married. She had fed herself the lie that all men were possessive, controlling jerks for far too long. It took Griff's kind and generous nature to change her heart.

It didn't hurt that he was easy on the eyes. Especially in that uniform.

Sarah glanced at her watch. "I didn't realize it was almost dinner time." Griff had just gotten off work.

"Why don't you come up to the main house for dinner, Gramps?" Griff offered. "I brought home your favorite from the diner." They had been doing a lot of takeout during the home renovations.

Gramps smiled. "If you don't mind, I'd love to take it here in my new home while I watch my shows."

Sarah smiled at Griff. "Of course. I'll bring it to you." Gramps was settling in, making the place his own. It did her heart good.

Griff and Sarah walked across the yard to their home. He threaded his fingers with hers and drew her close to him. His chest rose with a deep inhalation. "I never knew spring could smell so good."

Sarah filled her lungs and lowered her eyes in contentment. "How was work today?"

"Great. Best gig ever."

Griff was genuinely happy with this change of pace. She

had asked him a hundred times if he was sure being a Hunters Ridge sheriff's deputy was enough for him. He told her that everything—including her—had been more than he ever wanted. His mom also appeared to have adjusted to the idea of her only son working in the field instead of behind a desk. "After all, how much crime can go on around here?" she had once mused.

If only she knew.

"I helped the bishop round up his sheep. Someone left the gate open and they spilled out onto the road."

Sarah shook her head and smiled. "Oh, brownie points for me?"

Griff arched a brow. "That might be a stretch, but he did ask about Gramps."

Sarah hitched a corner of her mouth. "The bishop has the unenviable task of trying to keep the next generation in line. There are so many temptations in the outside world."

"True, but don't most of the kids grow up and remain with the Amish?" Griff asked as he held open the door to their new home. The smell of wood shavings and new paint held the promise of a home all their own.

A fuzzy furball bounded across the room and planted his paws on Sarah's knees. She reached down and patted her dog on his head. "I told you I wouldn't be gone long, didn't I?"

She never thought she'd be one of those people who talked to their pets in a singsong voice, but here she was. She and Griff had decided it was a no-brainer to take in the Gilmores' dog after Nicky's arrest.

"Yes, most do decide to be baptized Amish." She smiled tightly. "Even if the bishop gives me the side-eye every time I see him in town, I have forgiven him because Gramps has."

It was because of the bishop's harsh stance that Emma Mae had felt compelled to break into Sarah's office and steal her therapy notes. The bishop had spoken often—in front of

Emma Mae—that Sarah had counseled many of the Amish, including Hannah. He vowed that anyone seeking counsel from an outsider would be punished. He had no authority to access her clients' files, but it was the threat that drove Emma Mae. Hannah had known Emma Mae's secret, and Hannah had come to Sarah for help. If Emma Mae's secret was uncovered in those files, she'd be shunned until she came to her grandfather on bended knee. Considering the magnitude of her sin, she feared she'd face the shame for the rest of her life.

The thought of shaming the poor girl still made Sarah angry even as she worked on forgiveness. In the end, Gramps didn't want to press charges and the sheriff's department let it go. Sometimes things worked a little differently in small towns.

"Despite the bishop's stern warnings to the Amish youth, I'm still going to help whoever needs it." Sarah kept her shoes on to avoid stepping on any construction debris in the kitchen.

"I'll keep you safe," Griff said, coming up behind her and wrapping his strong arms around her waist.

She spun out from his grasp. It was her turn to give him the side-eye. "I can take care of myself, thank you very much."

Griff waggled his eyebrows. "I know you can, but isn't it nice to know you don't always have to?"

She planted a soft kiss on his warm lips.

A hammering sounded from the other room. She had forgotten that Timothy was still working. The new father needed money for his beautiful little boy.

Griff groaned and pulled away from Sarah. He leaned in to whisper. "We're going to continue this later."

A warm thrill coursed through her and she playfully patted him on the backside.

She strolled into the other room. "Looking good, Timothy. Think things will be ready by next week? Griff's niece is coming to stay for spring break."

"*Yah*," Timothy said. He pushed his hat back and scratched his head. His beard was growing in patchy. "I finished painting the smaller bedroom upstairs. The kitchen will take longer." A concerned look darkened his eyes.

"Lexi won't mind going out to eat. We just want a comfortable place for her to sleep," Griff said.

"She'll have it." Timothy bent and dipped his roller into the paint tray. "I'm going to work for a bit longer, then I better go. Emma Mae will be waiting for me."

"The baby sleeping any better?"

"*Yah.*"

"Good. I finished knitting a blanket." Sarah grabbed a gift bag from a closet off the main entryway. "Please bring it to her."

"*Denki.*" Thank you.

Sarah loved how Timothy didn't hesitate to use Pennsylvania Dutch in front of them. It made her feel like maybe their lives—the Plain and the Fancy, as she and Griff often joked—could live together and yet keep their respective beliefs.

"I still can't believe Lexi's coming," Griff said as he grabbed the broom to sweep up some of the construction dust.

"Better than going to a gymnastics competition in Scranton with her mother and little sisters."

"True."

Griff's sister had maintained custody of her girls upon the finalization of the divorce. After her experience with Nick Gilmore, Lexi grew up quick and had a new appreciation for her mother and her little sisters. And Sarah loved having an extended family. She looked forward to spending girl time with her new niece. Jeannie had insisted that Lexi loved to organize things and Sarah had figured there would be plenty to organize in their new home. If that wasn't enough spring break fun, Sarah and Griff promised to take her on a few college visits.

Sarah touched her belly, wondering if this was what it would be like when their kids were nearly grown. It was hard to imagine. Right now, all she felt was tired and happy.

Griff slipped his arms around her from behind and cradled her belly. "Maybe we should go to a motel until the painting is done."

Sarah had only taken the pregnancy test last night. The positive result came as a surprise. A very happy surprise. "I called the doctor. She said it was okay as long as we keep the windows open to air the place out." Sarah unfolded the top of the takeout bag. "What did you pick up?"

"Just what you asked for."

Sarah pulled out the BLT sandwiches wrapped in paper.

"Light mayo." He lifted a brow. "Pickle on the side."

"Thanks, I've been craving this all day."

Griff took the sandwich from her and put it down. She turned around in his arms and nestled her cheek on his solid chest. She never thought she could be so content. So happy.

With a gentle touch to her chin, he drew her face upward. He covered her lips with his and smiled. "I've been craving *this* all day." He gave her a quick peck and then playfully tapped her behind. "Eat before it gets cold. You're eating for two now."

Sarah laughed. "Does that mean I get your sandwich, too?"

Griff snatched his sandwich from the wrapper and took a big bite.

She reached over and wiped a glob of mayo from the corner of his mouth. "I thought you ordered light mayo."

"I did. But if the sandwich isn't to your liking, I'll run back to the diner." He kissed her above the ear and his breath tickled her neck.

"No, it's perfect," she whispered. *Everything's perfect.*

Absolutely perfect.

Turn the page for a sneak peek at Plain Revenge, the next book in the Hunters Ridge series.

SNEAK PEEK: PLAIN REVENGE

CHAPTER ONE

Nerves fluttered in Eve Reist's belly and immediately she felt like a teenager again as she turned onto the familiar country road. She had hoped she would have grown a backbone in the hour drive from her apartment, but if anything her unease grew. Her stomach cramped, she could barely swallow from lack of saliva, and she had the first tingling of what she suspected might explode into an all-out anxiety attack if she didn't rein in her emotions. *Fast.* She was usually good at calming herself, something she had to do on a regular basis before she went live on air as a reporter for a local news station in Buffalo. However, there weren't any cameras here in Hunters Ridge. Just her family.

The one she had abandoned seven years ago.

The August sun hung low in the sky and already she felt twitchy about arriving at this late hour, making her feel like the rebel Amish teen that she had once been. Eve had honestly intended to get on the road immediately after her last Sunday morning shift, but a creepy fan had other plans. Why would anyone think it was appropriate to leave a disturbing message on the windshield? Her stomach had bottomed out at the sight of the angry black strokes ghosting through the thin paper, similar to the one left on her car when she'd stopped at a department store a week earlier:

I'm watching you.

Eve forced herself to loosen her grip on the steering wheel as the familiar ache in her shoulder blades returned. The first note had made her hyperaware of her surroundings, and the second one had her totally questioning her career path. It had taken everything in Eve to act chill and pluck the note out from under the wiper and carry it over to Mark, the station's security guard, as if it were a dirty tissue. Despite the juvenile handwriting and unsophisticated means to harass her, the creep knew how to sneak in and out of the secure parking lot without being seen. The memory sent a new shudder up her spine even after the guard's promise to double-check for blind spots on the video feed and make the appropriate adjustments.

Eve squinted against the lowering sun and slowed to go around a horse and buggy. She found herself angling her face away from the Amish driver, fearing someone would recognize her.

Recognize me. Eve chuckled. That was the entire problem with being an on-air reporter. Her mentor, Carol Oliver, had told her that this was part of the job, as if it were no big deal. The lost sleep and racing thoughts suggested otherwise. Carol was a broadcasting legend in Buffalo. She retired years ago but maintained deep connections in the business and cashed in on her fame with a full schedule of speaking engagements. Eve could imagine her now responding to Eve's concerns with a lifted hand, an enormous diamond sparkling on a thin finger while she doled out some droll advice along the lines of: "When people invite you into their homes on their insanely large TVs, you have to expect some of this nonsense."

Expect it, maybe. Like it, definitely not.

Eve was grateful, at least, that the station had a protocol in place to monitor these kinds of situations—and tie-in with the local police when necessary—in an effort to keep their employees safe.

Butterflies swarmed in Eve's belly as her childhood home came into view at the top of the crest. The large white farmhouse had a wide front porch complete with rocking chairs and a swing. It would have been picturesque if it hadn't been wrought with so much personal, emotional baggage.

Eve pressed the brake and eased onto the side of the country road. She let out a slow breath and wondered if she'd be able to take care of everything in two weeks—her allotted vacation. She knew she could stretch it into four, if necessary, but that seemed like a long time to stay in Hunters Ridge. She drummed her thumbs on the steering wheel and stared up at the house. The sun reflected in an upstairs window making her wonder, not for the first time, about how things could have been so very different for the young Amish girl who went to sleep each night in that same bedroom. Closing her eyes briefly, she willed herself to relax. This wasn't going to be much of a vacation.

Realizing she couldn't avoid the unavoidable, Eve tapped the engine button and the country music on the radio that had kept her company on her drive and the AC fan cut out. The silence enveloped her. Something akin to shame made her cheeks burn. She hoped her return to Hunters Ridge hadn't come too late.

Eve pushed open the door of her compact sedan, and the humid air assaulted her at the same time as the sharp shrill of cicadas. Had it always been this loud? Her heart beat in her ears as she crossed the yard. The wood planks creaked as she climbed the steps to her childhood home.

A commotion sounded on the other side of the door that

made her pause and listen. Nostalgia, mixed with deep regret for all the time she had lost with her large Amish family, tightened like a band around her lungs, making it difficult to draw in a decent breath. Most of her siblings had grown and moved away to their own homes in Hunters Ridge or nearby Amish communities. However, her oldest brother, Thomas, and his children now occupied her former childhood home.

Mustering a strength that shouldn't have been this hard, considering they were her family, she finally knocked. The doorknob twisted and turned by some unseen hand.

"Let it alone, Jebediah." Her brother's deep, commanding voice reached out to her from an old memory, the harsh tone all too familiar. The door swung open, and a little boy who had merely been a speck in his mother's eye when Eve had fled Hunters Ridge slipped out onto the porch ahead of his father to inspect the stranger with narrowed eyes.

"Hello there." Eve smiled and pressed a hand to her favorite pink shirt that looked cute with her only pair of expensive jeans that she had so carefully selected from her limited wardrobe. She now realized how absolutely silly she had been. Anything other than a plain dress and bonnet would be an affront to her conservative, rule-following Amish brother. "I'm your—"

"Go inside." Her brother planted his hand on his son's head, gently turning him around and cutting short her introduction.

She swallowed hard and squared her shoulders. "Hello, Thomas." And then—unwilling to give him a chance to send her away—she added, "I came home to see *Mem.*" His silence made her heart race. "Is she here? Or should I try the *dawdy haus?*" She could have tried the smaller house on the property, but she had wanted to announce her presence and face her biggest fear first in order to squash it.

But it seemed her brother wasn't going to make it easy. A

muscle worked in his bearded jaw. A few strands of gray peppered his sandy brown beard despite him being only forty. Perhaps that was what being the father to six children did to a man. Thomas stepped fully onto the porch and pulled the door closed behind him. His expression softened for a fraction, as if he might be happy to see his long-lost sister, then his stern mask immediately settled back into place. "What are you doing here?"

"I came to visit Mother."

"Why now?" Suspicion sharpened his icy tone.

"It's time." Her niece Mercy had reached out to Eve to let her know Grandma Gerty was sick, but had begged Eve not to tell her father that she had called her.

Thomas seemed to be searching her face when the door opened behind him, first a fraction, then widely. Eve's heart exploded with affection and longing and shock. Her mother's round face had thinned and her bright eyes had hollowed. Leading with a cane she didn't need seven years ago, her mother stepped onto the porch. "Well, aren't you a sight for sore eyes." Her mother's voice cracked.

Tears immediately prickled the back of Eve's eyes. All the guilt and doubt and confusion at slipping away from Hunters Ridge in the middle of the night twisted like a garrote around her lungs.

"Hi, Mem." Eve stood rooted in place. A million questions clogged the back of her throat. Questions that would have to wait a hot second if she didn't want to betray Mercy's confidence.

"It's *gut* to see you." Her mother's lips quivered. Her papery-thin skin stretched across the bones of her thin face. Her faltering smile faded and she glared at her son. "Is this how you treat *die schweschder*?" Her mother lifted a shaky arm. "Come in. Abraham and Jebediah were about to play a board game with the girls, and I'm working on a quilt for

189

Mercy's hope chest." Abraham had been a little guy when she left.

Eve dipped her head and stepped inside and immediately felt the weight of all the stares from strangers. Her family. Mercy sat stock-still on the floor with two toddlers, no doubt her youngest siblings. The worry creasing her eyes suggested she didn't trust Eve to keep her secret. That she had been the one who had tracked down Eve. Since Eve had left the Amish, she had been placed under the *Bann*. Perhaps if the family shunned her, she'd feel the pressure to return on bended knee.

Mercy had only been eleven when Eve had left. She and Mercy had a special bond, and little Hazel, now fourteen, had been forbidden from tagging along on their adventures in the woods. All these years later, Eve hardly recognized her nieces who had blossomed into beautiful young women. Only now, in their presence, did she feel the full impact of what she had missed out on. It was easy to dismiss her upbringing and avoid the feelings of neglect from being shunned when she had created a busy life in the outside world. Surely they had to understand that. She only wanted to see her *mem*. She wasn't looking for forgiveness.

Grandma Gerty, as her grandchildren, then her entire family had lovingly called her, sat down heavily in the rocking chair closest to the wood-burning fireplace that stood unused in the August summer heat. She ran her hand over the fabric stretched taut in a large rectangular frame that looked much like a table covered with a tablecloth. In another life, Eve would have sat down across from her and picked up a needle.

Not today.

Thomas remained standing a few feet away from Eve, as if blocking her entry farther into the house. Her mother looked up. "Children, this is your Aunt Eve." The older woman lifted a shaky hand to the younger children who probably never knew their aunt existed. Turned out Grace and Gabriel, the twins, were only eighteen months old. Jebediah, named after her grandfather, was six. The rest of the children—Abraham now twelve, Hazel, fourteen, and of course, Mercy, eighteen—had remembered their aunt from her plain days. At least the girls did. Abraham's memories might have faded since Eve had been gone for more years of his life than she had been here.

One of the babies toddled over to Eve and grabbed onto her pant leg, struggling to get a grip on the thick fabric of her jeans. She bent down and brushed her fingers across the child's hair, damp from a bath, no doubt. "Well hello there, little one."

"Mercy," Thomas called his oldest daughter with a hard edge to his voice, "please collect Grace."

Mercy jumped up and sheepishly met Eve's gaze. She took her little sister's hand and led her back over to where the toddler's twin played with wooden blocks.

"I came here to see mother," Eve said, feeling her cheeks heat at the reality of what her visit was going to look like with her brother demanding his children shun their evil aunt. Her best friend, Suze Oliver, who happened to be Carol's daughter, would get a kick out of the fact that her wholesome, teetotaler friend was considered the wild one back home.

A twinge of guilt softened Eve's frustration. Thomas probably shouldered much of the blame for her departure, even if only in his mind. When Eve was sixteen, their father had died suddenly, making Thomas the man of the house. He had moved into their childhood home with his young family. Two short years later, Eve had jumped the fence in the middle of the night. She could only imagine how the tongues had wagged, blaming Thomas for not reining in his sister.

Jebediah, the six-year-old who had struggled to open the door when Eve arrived, had been hovering nearby and apparently worked up the nerve to speak. "You're our *aunt?*" The awe in his voice made her smile.

"Yes, I'm your *dat's* sister."

Jebediah furrowed his little brow. "How come I never met you? Why are you wearing fancy clothes? Are you going to live with us?" The boy peppered her with questions, not allowing her room to answer.

Thomas planted his palm on his son's head. "It's time for your bath. Go on now."

Jebediah gave her a long look, as if memorizing her, or maybe trying to figure out the answers no one seemed to want to give him.

Eve tracked his movement toward the kitchen where Katy, her sister-in-law, hung back, as if avoiding her. Even though it came as no surprise, it hurt. She had loved her brother's wife like an older sister. Eve felt a smile pull on her lips, a sad smile at everything she had missed. "Hello, Katy."

Her sister-in-law held out her hand to draw in her son. "Come on, Jeb. Time to get you cleaned up."

Eve stood in the middle of the room, uncomfortable with all the eyes on her. The itchy feeling was reminiscent of the nagging suspicion she sometimes had when she was live on camera and suddenly wondered if her lunch was stuck in her teeth. It was hard to imagine this had once been her home.

"How did you find out about…" Thomas let his words trail off, another crack in his stern demeanor. He took a step closer and asked her in confidence, "You came to see *Mem?* How did you know?"

Eve cut a gaze to her mother who was leaning heavily on the arm of the rocker, giving some quilting instructions to Hazel who had come to join her grandmother. Perhaps explaining the color choice or the best way to stitch. An immense feeling of nostalgia washed over her. Had it been that long ago that her mother—or her grandmother—had been teaching her the Amish fine arts? In Buffalo, she had taken up knitting, and her friends joked that she was like an old lady. What they didn't know was that she was trying to hang on to a piece of her childhood. Besides, the rhythmic motion and clacking of the knitting needles was soothing. A form of meditation.

"Eve?" Her brother pressed when she didn't answer.

"You of all people should know how gossipy Hunters Ridge is," Eve said, protecting her niece's secret. "*That's* how I found out that Mother's sick."

Read more. Find Plain Revenge on Amazon in ebook and paperback.

ALSO BY ALISON STONE

The Thrill of Sweet Suspense Series

(Stand-alone novels that can be read in any order)

Random Acts

Too Close to Home

Critical Diagnosis

Grave Danger

The Art of Deception

Hunters Ridge: Amish Romantic Suspense

The Millionaire's Amish Bride: Hunters Ridge Amish Romance

Plain Obsession: Book 1

Plain Missing: Book 2

Plain Escape: Book 3

Plain Revenge: Book 4

Plain Survival: Book 5

Plain Inferno: Book 6

Plain Trouble: Book 7

Plain Secrets: Book 8

A Jayne Murphy Dance Academy Cozy Mystery

Pointe & Shoot

Final Curtain

Corpse de Ballet

Bargain Boxed Sets

Hunters Ridge Book Bundle (Books 1-3)

The Thrill of Sweet Suspense Book Bundle (Books 1-3)

For a complete list of books visit

Alison Stone's Amazon Author Page

ABOUT THE AUTHOR

Alison Stone is a **Publishers Weekly bestselling author** who writes sweet romance, cozy mysteries, and inspirational romantic suspense, some of which contain bonnets and buggies.

Alison often refers to herself as the "accidental Amish author." She decided to try her hand at the genre after an editor put a call out for more Amish romantic suspense. Intrigued—and who doesn't love the movie *Witness* with Harrison Ford?—Alison dug into research, including visits to the Amish communities in Western New York where she lives. This sparked numerous story ideas, the first leading to her debut novel with Harlequin Love Inspired Suspense. Four subsequent Love Inspired Suspense titles went on to earn *RT magazine's TOP PICK!* designation, their highest ranking.

When Alison's not plotting ways to bring mayhem to Amish communities, she's writing romantic suspense with a more modern setting, sweet romances, and cozy mysteries. In order to meet her deadlines, she has to block the internet and hide her smartphone.

Married and the mother of four (almost) grown kids, Alison lives in the suburbs of Buffalo where the summers are gorgeous and the winters are perfect for curling up with a book—or writing one.

~

Be the first to learn about new books, giveaways and deals in Alison's newsletter. Sign up at AlisonStone.com.
Connect with Alison Stone online:
www.AlisonStone.com
Alison@AlisonStone.com

Made in the USA
Middletown, DE
04 May 2024

53861820R00120